The Preacher's Other Woman

By

Denora M. Boone

Dedication

This book like the last few is dedicated to
my later grandparents Dorothy and Fred Jefferson.
It's because of them I am the woman that I am

today. I love you and I hope I'm continuing to make you both proud.

Acknowledgements

First and foremost all praise and glory goes to God up above. If it wasn't for You sending Your precious Son to die on that cross for me I wouldn't be able to pen these stories that You give to me. Thank You for the gift of ministry through stories and I pray that You continue to use me for Your Kingdom.

To my amazing husband Byron, I don't know what I did for God to bless me with you but I sure am glad that you made me your wife. You are my protector and confidant and no matter how I feel you continue to love me and support me on this journey and I'm so grateful to you. I love you my King!

My babies Jalen, Elijah, Mekiyah, and Isaiah yall four push me to no end!! Lol!! You really do give mommy a run for my money but I wouldn't have it any other way. I do this so that the struggle Daddy and I have gone through you won't have to face. I want you to succeed long after we are gone and I'm going to do everything while we are here to make sure you all do! I love you!!

To my publisher David Weaver, you are definitely on my side. You been holding me down from the beginning and I thank you so much for going above and beyond to help me reach the success that God has for me. It's because of you that I am now a business owner and able to reach the goals that I have set for myself. I love and appreciate you because you are really family to me.

Boy this crew here knows that until I take my last breath I'm always here for them and that's my Anointed Inspirations Publishing family. You all make being your publisher a breeze and we have created such a strong bond because we all have the same vision and that's a Kingdom vision! Jenica Johnson and her husband Charles, Tabeitha Pollard Mann, my assistant Deedy Smith, and my new family members Andre Ray, Allison Randall Berewa, and Kathleen Richardson, thank you all so much for taking this journey with me. I can't wait to see all of the things that God has in store for you all through the gift of writing.

There are so many people that I would like to thank but God knows it's too many of yall but if you are in my life now I thank you. If you have ever been in my life, I thank you. And for whoever that is coming into my life in the future I thank you in advance! Now let's see what shenanigans this Pastor is up to! Enjoy!!!

Follow me on social media

Twitter: @mzboone27

@a_i_p

Instagram: @mzboone81

Facebook:
https://www.facebook.com/denora.boone

Chapter One

Drew

I put the last of my underwear in my suitcase and zipped it up on the bed before walking over to get my toiletries off of my dresser. As I passed by the floor length mirror in my bedroom I couldn't help but to admire the man that was looking back at me.

I stood a cool 6'3 with blemish free milk chocolate skin that covered my solid build. I made sure to keep my hair cut low and tapered on the sides. The waves in my hair would cause anyone to get seasick if they stared at them a second too long. I had been lucky enough to inherit my grandmother's hazel green eyes that seemed to change with my mood. One day GQ Magazine would find me and I would grace their cover and pages but until then I would just grace the lives of the women who loved me.

Modeling should have been my career choice but instead I was the lead pastor of my wife's family church. Her grandfather had left it to her and her brother Chris, but he was far from trying to be a man of the cloth. Once we got married her father thought it would be a good idea for me to take over that position. And who I was I to not walk in the calling that was on my life.

The calling on my life. That was still a joke to me but the joke was about to be on everybody else soon. In less than three weeks the day after my ten year anniversary of being in ministry I would be on a plane to the islands with a bank account full of money. It tripped me out how every Sunday I could deliver such a powerful word on behalf of the Lord and have people falling all out on the floor. I heard the voice of God warning me on the regular. He often used my best friend Bryce to warn me and even a few of the elders in the church but I wasn't there for that. I was there to get what I had owed to me and I wasn't leaving without it. Ten years had been a long time for me to walk away with nothing. Nah I was about to have it all and I couldn't wait.

"You got everything babe?" my wife Jewel asked me as she came up behind me putting her arms around my waist. I'm glad that from the angle she stood behind me she couldn't see when I rolled my eyes. The tone of my voice surely didn't match the expression I had on my face at the time.

"Yep. I'm all ready to go forth on God's behalf and speak to His people." I said.

It amazed me that I knew the word of God like I did but hey the devil knows the word too. He was once an angel of light before he got kicked out of heaven.

"I wish me and the girls were going with you this time."

"Mmm hmmm me too babe." I said lying once again through my straight pearly white teeth.

"I'm going to check on the girls before Bryce gets here." I said removing her chunky arms from my body. Don't get me wrong my wife Jewel had a pretty face but I just wasn't into the pleasantly plump ladies.

Jewel wasn't short but she wasn't tall and the weight that her body carried was in all of the wrong places. But she did have a beautiful face. A deep caramel complexion, long brown hair that she kept in flowing curls, no weave for her. Her eyes were so big and bright and held an innocence in them that I admired. It just wasn't enough to make me interested or faithful. I had one mission being married to her and it wasn't love. The only reason we had two daughters was because I had to make this marriage seem legit to so many people and I was still a man. When the lights went out it was all the same to me anyway.

I walked out on Jewel as she just stood there looking crazy and headed down the hall. My oldest daughter Avery wasn't in her room so I headed to my baby girl's room. Had my heart been set up to be a family man for real this would have been the ideal environment for me. I couldn't get with it though.

"Hey baby girl what you doing?" I asked my youngest daughter Kammy as I walked into her room. I was about to head out of town for the next two weeks and I wanted to make sure that I spent as much time with her as I could. I was headed to Atlanta to be a guest speaker at Living Word Tabernacle.

Well at least that was what I had told my wife Jewel and our two daughters. I was actually going to be speaking for one night and the rest of the time I was spending with my little side piece. So this time my family wouldn't be coming with me on *assignment*.

Sure I was a preacher but I was still a man that loved women. I don't care how well my wife took care of home or how sweet my daughters were it wasn't enough. It amazed me how I had a woman, sometimes two, in almost every state and my wife was oblivious to the fact. From my understanding women were supposed to have some kind of intuition about things like this but I guess Jewel lacked that ability like she lacked self-esteem.

Jewel was far from a bad mother and wife but I wasn't attracted to her. Never have been too much when I think about it. I met her when we were in college. I attended Clark Atlanta and she was at Spellman. We had *bumped* into one another at a campus party one night and me already knowing who she was I ended up asking her out on a date.

She was on the heavy side and dressed in big clothes that did nothing for the shape she didn't have. It was just a mess but never the less I had a mission to complete.

"Daddy did you hear me?" My six year old said getting my attention looking up from her doll that she was pretending to feed. I'm sure if I gave it some effort I could love everything about this little girl. From her long black hair, to her honey colored eyes, and right down to her toothless smile.

"I'm sorry baby I was thinking to make sure I had everything I needed. I'm about to leave for the airport Stink." I told her calling her by the nickname that I gave her as a baby.

I saw the sadness wash over her before she said,

"Aww Daddy do you have to go?"

"Yes sweetie. I thought you understood when we had our little talk the other night." I said walking over to her and sitting down on the floor. No sooner than I had gotten comfortable she hopped in my lap and put her head on my shoulder.

"I did but I prayed to God for you not to go." She said with water beginning to form in her eyes. This was the hard part about living this life. Although I wasn't really the fatherly type like I should have been I put on a good front and I did hate to see her get like this.

"Well baby I'm going so that I can go talk to God's people. He has a message that He wants me to give them." I explained to her.

"Well can't you call them and tell them?" she pouted.

"That would be a lot of people to call baby." I answered her with a laugh.

"I'll help. I can use Mommy's phone to call them with you." Kammy said with hope displaying on her beautiful brown face. She was just not letting this go.

"Mom said Uncle Bryce is here to take you to the airport." My daughter Avery said coming into the room before I could respond to Kam.

"Let her know I'll be right there." I said as she turned and walked away without another word.

"How about this" I started turning back around to give my baby my full attention again, "When I get back we can take a trip somewhere nice."

"Disney World!" she asked jumping up and down in my lap.

"Sounds good to me but you have to be on your best behavior for Mommy while I'm gone. Deal?" I asked holding out my hand for her to shake it. I almost felt bad

that she wouldn't be going on this trip to see Mickey and

the crew. Oh well her mother would dry her tears.

Instead of her answering me right away she put her

pointer finger up to her lips and looked to the ceiling as if

she was in deep thought and finally said, "Deal!"

I kissed her on her forehead before getting up to go

get my bags and head downstairs.

"Ugh I can't stand him!" I heard Avery say as I

walked past her room. I wasn't even going to entertain her

today but the feeling was definitely mutual. It seemed like

ever since that child came into this world we have never

gotten along. Every time I got close to her or tried to pick

her up she would scream and holler like someone was

killing her.

The older she got the worse it got to where I just stopped

trying.

Avery wouldn't listen to anything I said and if her mother wasn't around we would not have a conversation. From the rolling of the eyes to the stomping of her feet whenever I addressed her, we just did not get along. I often heard the old people when they would say that a baby or a small child could tell if a person had a good spirit or not. Because of the way Avery responded to me was like she had known all along what I had done and one day I was going to pay severely for that.

Chapter Two

Drew

I got my bags and headed downstairs to meet up with my boy Bryce who was also my personal assistant and minister at my father-in-law's church. Bryce and I had been friends since the second grade when he moved from Philly to Charlotte. He was a little rough around the edges and as soon as he walked into Mrs. Patterson's class I knew we would get along well.

"What's good bro?" he asked as I entered the kitchen.

"Why is it every time you come over here man you end up eating up all of my food?" I ignored his question and asking one of my own while I laughed.

"Man listen. Sis offers and it would be rude to decline. Besides you know I'm a single man and don't have the luxury of a beautiful wife cooking for me every night." He said looking over at Jewel and winking at her.

She didn't respond but I could have sworn she was blushing when she looked away. Not sure what that was about but I was going to leave it alone for now. Trust and believe the truth always came out.

Bryce wasn't a bad looking guy he was the exact opposite. This cat had the women beating down his door since the day I met him. Sometimes he would have to beat them off with a stick. He was the star football player throughout his high school career and the girls loved a jock but that wasn't his dream. I never understood how he did the things we did together but had a dream of one day becoming a minister. That was so backwards to me.

The women loved his six foot frame with broad shoulders and dark skin. He put you in the mind of that actor Lance Gross but he was just a little bigger. Lance needed to come by the house and let Jewel get down one time for him in the kitchen and he and Bryce could have been twins. Bryce didn't keep his hair low like I did instead he kept it close on the sides and naturally curly on the top.

When Jewel and I were talking about marriage and taking over the church I asked him to come with me to help me run it and he jumped at the chance. I also needed him there with me to help cover up what I was doing. I trusted Bryce with everything but he didn't know the real reason to why I was in this marriage and he would never find out. I was glad that he didn't have a wife or kids to tend to because if I needed him to intercept something I was doing he was available. That was my boy through and through and I knew that although he constantly told me to leave the women alone he wouldn't say a word. His loyalty was to me and to me only.

"Come on man before I miss my flight." I said picking up my carryon and walking over to my wife.

"Here are all of your reservations for the flight, hotel, and car baby. Be careful and make sure you call me as soon as you land ok." She said to me as she handed me everything.

This is one of the reasons that I put up with Jewel as a person. She took care of any and everything that I needed without me even asking her to do it. If it wasn't for her I don't know where I would be right now. It was because of her that I was finally able to be in the position that I am now.

"Thank you baby. What would I do without you in my life?" I asked her pulling her close to me. I held her so close that I could feel the pulse of her beating heart through her blouse.

"You would probably crash and *burn.*" She said as a look I had never seen on her beautiful brown face appeared and disappeared just as fast.

Bryce cleared his throat as I turned to look at him. He wouldn't make eye contact with me and I already knew what that was about. It wasn't something we were going to discuss right now but on the way to the airport I was sure we would have the same conversation we often had.

"You better hurry up before you miss your flight. I love you baby and be careful." Jewel said giving me a long deep kiss.

"Keep this up First Lady and I'm not going anywhere but upstairs." I said gassing her up. I couldn't wait to get out of this house.

"Boy bye!" she giggled like a little school girl.

"Let's go bro. Kingdom business awaits." I said grabbing my things and walking out.

"Wait!" Jewel called out behind us before we were able to get out of the door. I didn't know why it felt like my heart had dropped to my knees.

"Yea bae?" I asked giving her my full attention.

"Bryce do you have everything you need for this trip this time? I am not going to be running around trying to overnight you anything this go round." She laughed but Bryce didn't. He looked nervous to even respond but I guess the heat coming from my stare made him realize that he better say something and fast.

"Now sis you know I'm prepared unlike this one here?" he tried to play it off while nudging me with his elbow.

"Mmm hmm. Yall be safe." Was her reply as she ushered us out the door and kissing me one last time.

I didn't know what was going on but something was off and it now had my spirit unsettled.

******

"Hey man what was that all about?" I turned to my best friend and asked as we got on the highway heading to Charlotte Douglas International Airport to catch my flight.

"What?" he asked me with a shrug of his shoulders.

"You know what I'm talking about. All of those little slick comments and eye movements." I asked finding myself getting angry on the inside and I didn't know why.

"Whoa? I know you not thinking I'm trying to get at J." he said getting defensive with a look of hurt on his face.

"Nah man. My bad. It's just so much going on these days." I apologized.

"Yea. I bet." Was all he said before turning up the radio as K Camp rapped about turning up for a check.

Don't get it twisted we both loved the Lord and could quote the word of God forwards and backwards but we were still as real as they came. Being saved didn't mean we had to walk around listening to gospel or constantly quoting scriptures all day long. There had to be a balance.

"Hey man." Bryce said turning the music back down as he made his way down the highway.

"What's up?" I asked already sensing where this conversation was headed.

"When you gonna stop this? I know it has to be draining you." He asked glancing at me then back at the road.

"Stop what? Ministering on the road so much? You know I can't sit still in one city when there are so many hurting souls out there that's needing a word from God." I laughed at myself. Even to me that explanation sounded ridiculous.

"You know good and well that's not what I'm referring to."

"Just say it then bruh."

"The women. When are you going to finally come clean and stop doing Jewel like this? Her and those girls don't deserve to be treated like that. You have two daughters to think about. Do you want them growing up to have some lil knucklehead doing them like you are doing their mother?" he asked giving me an earful.

I sat there for a minute thinking about what he had just said and tried letting it sink in. For some reason it just wasn't registering in my head or my heart enough for me to stop.

"Listen B. We been doing this since high school and you know good and well I'm too young to stop now. Heck you taught me the game." I replied while reminding him who watered the seed that my father had already planted in me years ago.

I saw my father Andrew, Sr. do my mother the same way and she knew about all of the other women. She didn't leave, my mother stayed right there through it all.

"Nah. Pops taught you the game I just helped you to perfect it." He said chuckling. "But on the real, it was all fun and games when we were single but you're a married man with little girls man. The reason I'm still single is because I want to find the right one and settle down. We are getting too old to keep this up." He said calling himself schooling me.

"Speak for yourself bruh. I'm just getting started." Noticing we had finally arrived at the airport. "Don't forget to stay away from the house until I get back. Jewel thinks you are going with me this time around."

"Maaannnn." He started.

"You got me or not B?" I asked already knowing the answer.

It took him a few seconds to answer as he looked out of the driver's side window. He had always been down no matter what but now it seemed like he was changing on me. Like he was finally getting a conscience.

"Well?" I asked getting somewhat impatient.

"Yeah man. I got you." He sighed.

"My boy. I'll hit you up later on this evening once I get settled." I let him know as I opened the back door to get my bags. Without another word as soon as I shut the door he drove off.

"*It's time to stop this son.*" I heard and looked around to see if there was anyone around me. Even though I knew it wasn't the voice of one of the people passing by.

I knew the voice of God and I knew it well. I heard it often these days and just like so many other people I continued to ignore it. I had a life to live and I was going to live it the way I wanted. And right now I wanted to get to Atlanta to Jasmine.

Chapter Three

Jewel

Looking out of the living room window I watched as Bryce drove my loving husband away. I thanked God for him each and every day that I woke up even if he wasn't always next to me in bed when my eyes opened. I knew that the position he was in caused him to be gone a lot but that was the sacrifice that had to be made when you were married to a preacher.

It took a toll on us all but when he was finally able to be home, which wasn't too often, he made us feel like we were the only people in the world. Although Kammy loved her father I never could understand why Avery was the way she was when it came to Drew. She bucked against his authority for as long as I could remember and no matter how much he tried to talk to her she would always shut down. I just prayed that before she went out on her own after high school their relationship would be better.

I went into the kitchen to clean up the dishes that Bryce had left and found Avery standing with the refrigerator wide open. I hated when she did that but no matter how many times I got on to her she still did it.

"Little girl what have I told you about standing with that door open?" I asked startling her.

"Mommy you scared me!" she exclaimed grabbing a cold Pepsi and a fruit cup.

"Well if you weren't doing something you had no business then you wouldn't have gotten scared." I said getting the dishes off of the island and placing them in the dishwasher.

"Ma can I ask you something?" Avery said hopping up on the bar stool that Bryce had just been on.

"Of course baby. What's going on?" I asked looking at her face that was full of concern.

I always taught both Avery and Kammy that they could come to me about any and everything no matter what it was. I felt it was so important that kids were able to be open to their parents these days.

"Ma why do you stay?" she asked me with tears in her eyes.

This question threw me way off because I had no clue what she was talking about.

"Av what are you talking about?" I asked confused.

"Why do you stay with Dad? He doesn't love you and you deserve so much better."

"Wait a minute, I'm lost. Why wouldn't I stay with him? He's my husband and your father."

"It takes more to being a husband than a ring and more to being a father than having a long stroke."

"AVERY MONIQUE WEBBER!" I yelled startling her. There weren't many times that I had to yell at my children but when I did they knew I was serious. I don't know what had gotten into her lately but she was definitely about to get whatever it was casted out.

"I'm sorry." She said as a tear slid down her face.

I softened up just a little because if there was anything I hated it was to see my children hurt.

"I'm sorry for yelling." I said sitting back down. "Talk to me please. I hate seeing you cry."

"I don't think Dad is really in love with you. I mean I know that he loves you but I don't think it's the way that he should."

"We have been together almost twenty years baby girl. Why wouldn't he?" I wanted to know.

"Just because you are with someone that long doesn't mean that they love you the way you love them." She said. I was at a loss for words so she continued.

"I know I've only been on this earth for seventeen years but I can't remember a time that he has looked at you with as much love in his eyes for you as you have for him. Sometimes I wonder if you are just settling with him to have someone and a father for us. You deserve better than this Ma." She finished and got up and headed upstairs leaving me there to think about what it was that she had just said.

As I sat there I began to think about if there was any truth to what she was saying. Was I settling with Drew because I was afraid for us to be alone? I know I hadn't always had the best self esteem growing up but to have my own daughter call me out on it was a shock. At that moment I understood how so many people, including myself, couldn't see things that were going on right in front of their faces until God sent someone to open their eyes. It caused me to take a good look at my past and how I got to this point in my life

*****

1997

The time had finally come and I was about to walk into Spellman for the first time. I had just graduated high school and couldn't have been any happier than I was at this moment. To finally be getting out of that small behind town of Sparta, Georgia. It wasn't that I didn't love the people I had grown up with but I was ready to see and do more and Sparta just wasn't going to afford me that opportunity.

As excited as I was to embark on this new journey I was so nervous. I hadn't been the most popular girl at Hancock Central High and my attitude reflected that. I wanted so bad to be accepted by the in crowd but it just never happened. I didn't fit in. My parents often told me how beautiful and smart I was but I wanted someone else to tell me that. Parents are supposed to tell their children things like that so it was expected.

I had a few girlfriends that I would talk to while in school but it never went beyond that. No sleepovers, mall outings, or even phone calls. My appearance wasn't horrible but it wasn't the best either. My parents weren't rich but they made sure my brother Chris and I had what we needed.

Our parents were ministers at our local church and did their best to instill values in us. We were always taught that clothes didn't make the person but it was what God had placed inside of us that mattered. That was all good and well but the way kids at school would pick at me because of the clothes I wore had a big impact on me.

Whoever came up with that phrase that bigger is better lied. Because my height didn't compliment my weight I just looked round. No matter how cute I thought an outfit was when my mother took me shopping once I put it on it looked nothing like I imagined. So I got picked on. I hated when I heard, "You have a cute face for a big girl." Like big girls were exempt from being pretty just because they had a little more weight on their bodies.

I was so self-conscience about myself and hated being beat down mentally every day I walked into that school that my senior year I asked to be home schooled. My Dad tried to tell me that running away from an issue was never good because until you passed that test you would have to keep facing it until you did. College wasn't even on my mind because I felt like things were only going to get worse. I should have listened to my gut when it told me not to go but I let my mother convince me to step out on faith and trust this experience would be the best thing for me.

So here I am. No turning back now. Chris had just brought up the last box with my dad as my mother and I tried our best to organize the mess. Just as we were finishing up a pretty light skinned girl came walking through the door. Immediately I looked down at myself and started comparing myself to her.

She was light skinned and I was about two shades darker than a paper bag. Her hair was styled in a pretty French roll with pin curls while mine was struggling to stay in the pony tail holder. It wasn't that I was bald but I had so much hair that I couldn't maintain it so it just stayed in a bun. We were both about the same height of five foot six but while she was a nice stacked one hundred and forty pounds, give or take, I was a hefty two hundred and ten.

Both of us were dressed in t-shirts and jean shorts but she made hers look so much better. My thighs rubbed together while hers were an even distance apart. I knew I had probably made her uncomfortable by just staring at her for so long but I was questioning God wondering why I had to look the way that I did. I wasn't a big eater or anything and I tried my best to work out but the results weren't in my favor.

"Um. Hi. I'm Jasmine Hawkings." My new roommate said extending her hand for me to shake.

"Oh I'm so sorry. I'm Jewel and this is my mother and father Pastor and First Lady Rivers and my brother Chris." I said introducing her to my family.

"Well we are going to go ahead and head back home. I am so proud of you baby girl and don't you hesitate t call us if you need anything." My dad said

walking over to me and giving me one of his bear hugs that I was going to miss so much.

"I will Daddy." The tears were on the verge of falling freely at any moment.

"No ma'am none of that. We are not that far away and we will definitely see you on the weekends." My mother encouraged.

Before they left my father decided that it would be a good idea to pray. So we all held hands including Jasmine while he asked our Father in heaven to watch over and protect us while we were away from home. Each one of us said Amen and they were on their way.

*****

The first week of classes went by without a hitch and I was trying my hardest to come out of my shell. The more I hung with Jasmine and got to know her the more she pushed me to be better. I had let her so far into my life and she had done the same that we started telling people we were sisters. She even helped me to change up my look some. We would go shopping and she would let me in on all of the latest trends and hair styles. No matter how good I looked on the outside my inside was still a mess.

One night we were hanging around in our room listening to music and studying when out of nowhere Jasmine asked me about my love life.

"What love life?" I asked hoping and praying that she didn't pry but that prayer didn't go any further than the ceiling.

"You mean to tell me that you never had a boyfriend?" she questioned while closing her sociology book and sitting up on her bed to face me.

"Well yea but it didn't work out." I replied. Something told me that this wouldn't be the end of her interrogation.

"What happened?"

I was right again.

"I met him my sophomore year of high school and fell hard for him way too fast. After a few months Romeo asked if we could take our relationship to the next level."

"Wait his name was not Romeo for real was it? I know his mama did not put that on his birth certificate." She said as she fell out laughing.

"Girl yes!" I said giggling with her.

"Go ahead and finish telling me what happened before I die from laughing so hard."

"Anyway. You know I was raised up in the church and premarital sex was frowned upon. When I told him that I wanted to save myself for marriage he laughed in my face and told me that he would never stoop that low and sleep with someone that looked like me. It was just a game to him and all of that time I spent with him thinking that he was really loving me like I was loving him was all a waste of time." I ended as Jasmine got up and held me while I cried.

"So I haven't been with anyone else since then. That's why I try so hard to lose this weight and change my image because I really want to just be happy and find love."

"Don't worry sis the man God has for you will one day find you."

"I hope so. I really hope so." I said focusing back on my school work.

Chapter Four

Jewel

I hadn't realized that I had gone down memory lane until I heard my cell phone ringing on the counter. I ran over to it and caught Drew's call right before he hung up.

"Hey baby." I said almost out of breath.

"Hey what's wrong? Sounds like you been running a marathon and we know that's not happening." He laughed.

Maybe I missed the joke but I didn't find that comment one bit amusing. Something wasn't right and this was the first time he has ever made me feel insecure about my size. I guess he realized he had hurt me and tried to correct himself.

"Oh no baby not like that. I didn't mean it to come off like that." He tried to clean it up.

"So you made it in safely?" I asked him trying to change the subject.

"Yep but I have to end up crashing at a buddy's house." He said nonchalantly.

"That's strange what happened? I had you all booked and ready to check in once you landed."

"Well when I got here I was told that they overbooked so instead of causing a scene I just hit one of my college buddies up to see if I could crash there. It's no big deal, he was fine with it."

"Oh that was nice. Which friend was it?" I asked as my stomach started doing flips. Normally I wouldn't think twice about it because there were times that this has happened. But lately I've been feeling something has been off between us.

"You don't know him. I'll call you back later on tonight I gotta go. Bye." He said before hanging up in my face.

"I love you too." I said although he was no longer there.

I put my phone down just as the tear that I had been holding on to for the last seven years rolled down my face.

"Mommy why are you crying?" I heard my little princess Kammy say. I was so into my own thoughts I didn't even hear her come in.

"Oh it's nothing baby girl." I said looking down into her pretty brown face. She reminded me of a little porcelain doll. Kamiah Noel was a gorgeous little girl but her heart and personality made her beautiful inside as well.

"Why does everyone keep saying that to me?" she asked pouting her lips.

If I didn't know she was so serious I would have laughed at her because she was so cute. But I wanted to know what she meant by that statement.

"What do you mean Kam?"

"When I ask Daddy why he looks at you a certain way when you aren't looking he tells me it's nothing. I just saw Avey crying in her room and I asked what was wrong but she smiled and said nothing and now you too Mommy."

I was at a loss for words and didn't know where to begin. It amazed me that this child of mine was only six years old but seemed to be very observant. So observant that she was noticing things that I should have been seeing in my own home. I didn't know what God had in store but He was definitely trying to get my attention. I just didn't know why right now.

"Come here sweetie." I said as I picked her up in my arms and sat her on the counter.

"Mommy is sorry. I don't want you to think we aren't being honest with you or hiding things from you. But some things that we go through may be just a little too much for you to handle or understand at your age." I tried to explain to her but what she said next knocked the breath out of me.

"I understand that Daddy doesn't love us." She said without an ounce of emotion on her face.

"Kammy why would you say that? Your father loves us."

"No he doesn't Mommy. It's ok though because God has prepared my heart and He said He will prepare yours too."

Once again another one of my children left me speechless. Getting down off of my lap she gave me a hug and kiss before skipping off and heading up the stairs to her playroom.

Chapter Five

Jasmine

The club was packed and bodies were everywhere. I hated it. For the men it was a place to get a free feel and maybe something extra if they paid enough to the woman they set their sights on. One after another the women hit the stage in barely anything at all just to make a few dollars to get them to the next day. Some even made enough in a few minutes for the whole month but they were back at it the next night to do it all over again.

This wasn't the life I wanted to have but the one I wanted was already occupied by someone else. That wouldn't be for long though and everything I worked so hard for would surely be mine in the end. We put in too many years of planning for this to not work. Jasmine Ray was about to become Mrs. Andrew "Drew" Webber.

Believe that! My son was about to have both of his parents at home together and in love unlike how I grew up. My prayers were finally about to be answered and I had God and my so called best friend Jewel to thank for that. Before I had the chance to dwell on those thoughts anymore I heard the intro to the song for my next set.

Exit Jasmine and enter Onyx. I had gained a little weight over the years but in all the right places unlike some people. Staying in shape wasn't an issue for me because the pole life was nothing but daily exercise. The bundles of Malaysian body wave that I had just gotten sewn in fell right in the dip of my back where my all natural fatty began. My face was beat to perfection and the rest of my body was on point as usual. The girls sat up nice and high, my abs were covered in baby oil and glistened under the lights, and my thighs were tight and right. Yep I was a bad one and Drew knew that from the first time his eyes landed on me.

"What you know bout the grind in the streets

He move and work out of town every week

I know about it

I know about it

What y'all know bout them girls on the pole

She make her money every night, taking off

her clothes

I know about it

Yep I know about it oh

'Cause all my life I've been struggling and

stressing

That's why I come up in this piece with

aggression

Where I'm from, niggas die every day

Bet you ain't never seen a nigga die in your

face

The life the life, the sacrifice

The grind and the grind you get sometimes

I know about it

Don't judge if you know nothing bout it

We try and try to live it right

But we get blinded by the light, oh oh

I know about it"

K Michelle and Meek Mill filled the speakers throughout the club with the soundtrack to my life. If this didn't describe me to the tee I didn't know what did. Jasmine was the girl that wanted more and had the education and brains to get there but no one wanted to recognize that in me. So it was Onyx that got their attention. Onyx was the no nonsense get it how you live chick.

See I didn't have the type of parents that cared about my education enough to save up for me to go to college. I had to do that on my own unlike my roommate Jewel. She had it all. Her parents weren't filthy rich but they made sure her and her brother were good. When I first met them our freshman year of college I initially liked her but when I started to see how low her self esteem was it irked me to no end. I just couldn't understand how she could have this loving Christian family who supported her with everything she decided to do but she was still unhappy. Had it been me I would have been all smiles.

Don't get it twisted Jewel was a pretty girl to be on the heavy side but dudes weren't checking for her back then. Once she told me that the reason she felt so bad about herself I kind of lost respect for her. There was no way that any man could make me feel bad about myself. I had never been big but I know that no one can make me feel less than what I am. Forget that. She had it all and didn't even see it and I didn't care enough after that to let her know. I actually found it quite comical. The night she broke down everything about who she was and what her parents expected out of her in order to get an inheritance, I knew I had to put a plan in motion so that I could live that life.

I finished my set and went to the back to count the money I made for the night. A funky two grand was all that I walked away with so I knew that I was going to have to work the floor tonight as well and do some private dances in order to get the full five that I wanted. There were some red bottoms I had my eyes on at Lennox Mall and I couldn't wait on my man to buy them. Drew was taking care of all of my bills and our son DJ but the extra things that I wanted right away I had to get myself for the time being until he was finally all mine. It was easy for Drew to tell Jewel that the things he was paying for with the church money was for different families in the congregation or other people that needed the church's assistance in the community. Part of it was true, he was helping those people, but his true love and son were getting taken care of as well.

Jewel was so stupid that she trusted everything that he told her without even checking behind him. Had that been me, babyyy I would have asked to see receipts for everything he paid for all the way down to his draws and socks! Soon this would all be over with though. At least that's what I hoped and prayed for. I had let Drew in on what I knew about her inheritance and he was only supposed to be with her for just a few years. He was to earn her trust, get her pregnant and stay married to her for five years in order to receive whatever it was that her grandfather had left her. When that time came I asked why hadn't he left he told me that it wouldn't look right and that he had to stay just a little while longer to make it believable. I was cool with that at first but here we are almost eighteen years later and I was tired of waiting. I wanted my family and whatever it was that was a part of that inheritance.

I knew that Drew was on his way to Atlanta for the next two weeks so I was going to make sure I gave him any and everything he wanted while he was here. I wanted him to know when he left this time that he had until the church anniversary to come clean or I was going to let Jewel know exactly what had been going on right under her nose. I mean my so called best friend and God daughters deserved to know the truth finally. Drew may be mad at first but since I knew this was where he wanted to be and our bank account would be looking lovely, he would get over it real fast.

Chapter Six

Avery

Chris Brown was singing about how these girls these days weren't loyal to the dudes they were with but someone needs to talk about how these men aren't either. I don't know how my mother couldn't see what her husband was doing right under her nose. I used to look at some of the girls at school and think love couldn't make you blind like that but about a year ago I started understanding why. My mother was just like them and I couldn't stand it.

I prayed nightly that when I did find a boyfriend he wouldn't treat me like the boys at school and most importantly nothing like my so called father. He would come in some nights so late the sun was about to come up then there were some nights he wouldn't even come home at all. Ministry was what he called it but I knew better and for the life of me didn't know how my mom was so oblivious.

The first night that I can remember him coming home late was the night I lost the little respect for him that I had. I was so tired from studying but I had to make an A on this upcoming Honors Algebra exam I was about to take the next morning. Mom had gone to bed about nine o'clock because she had been planning a women's conference and it had started taking its toll on her body. That's one thing I admired about her, she was such a go getter for God and her family. She worked hard for us and I loved her for that.

Kammy was in bed watching Frozen and could barely hold her eyes open. I knew she was waiting on either mommy or myself to come tuck her in. I walked into her room and went over to her princess canopy bed and got under the cover with her. I loved my little sister and knew that she looked up to me so I had to make sure I was a good role model for her. Kam slid closer to me and put her head on my shoulder and soon after she began to lightly snore. I turned off her tv and turned on her night light. If she didn't have it on and woke up in the middle of the night she would freak out.

Making sure she was tucked in I headed out of her room and down the hall to mine. I loved my personal space. It was decorated in purple and silver. My queen size bed was covered in a shimmery purple comforter set with silver accents. There was a 42" inch television on the wall across from the bed and I had my computer desk in front of my bay window. Even my carpet was a fluffy purple material that I loved to sink my toes into.

Turning off my overhead light I made my way over to the bed where I left my laptop and cellphone. I had missed a text from my friend James that lived in Georgia. I met him at one of the vacation Bible school camps that we attended each year. It was his first year since moving in with his father who was also a pastor and his step mother. James and his little brother JJ had been through so much and my heart went out to them. He was so sweet and I could tell him everything without feeling like I was being judged. I sent him a simple text back letting him know that I had just put Kam to bed and was about to study but I would call him tomorrow.

Placing my phone on the charger I started to climb in the bed but before I could I heard a car door shut. I knew that Dad wasn't home because I didn't hear the garage door come open so I got up to peek outside. I wasn't worried about someone noticing me because with my light off you couldn't see my shadow. The closer I got to my window the harder my heart seemed to beat. I had no idea what I was about to see but right before I slid my curtain to the side I felt a sense of calmness. Like God was wrapping His arms around me at that very moment so that I would keep calm about whatever it was I was about to face. I felt that feeling often when things were tough for me and it got me through.

I opened my window and prayed that God would let my mother and sister feel that calmness and protection from God once He revealed to them what I was looking at. The woman that was standing in front of my father I couldn't recognize but from the look on his face he knew exactly who she was. They were parked right in our driveway like this was their house instead of the house he shared with his family.

The woman put her arms around him and they kissed long and hard before she got in his car and drove away. Once she was out of sight he turned around and walked towards our front door. As my heart shattered and the tears ran down my face my phone began to vibrate on the nightstand. I walked over to it and without looking to see who it was I answered.

"Hello?" I said in a raspy voice.

"Ave? That you?" I heard James ask me.

"Yeah it's me."

Tears were beginning to flow so rapidly and the anger setting in that I didn't realize I had begun hyperventilating.

"Avery calm down. You're gonna pass out if you don't calm your breathing." He said to me in his deep baritone voice.

"How could he do this to her?" I said not necessarily to James but more to myself.

"Listen Avery I know it's late, I don't know what's going on but God lead me to pray for you tonight before I go to bed. If that's okay,"

"Yeah. Fine." My thoughts were all over the place and I wanted so bad to go wake my mom up and tell her what I just saw. But as upset as I was I knew that she wasn't in the right mind frame to deal with him and his shenanigans just yet.

"Avey I want you to close your eyes and take your focus off of anything that's going on around you. I need you to close your eyes and focus on God. God I'm not sure the issues that are going on at the present moment but we know You are able to do the impossible. God I'm asking that you begin to wrap Avery in Your arms and let her know that what she sees is only the work of you. Let her know God that all things will work together for her and family's good because they are lovers of you.

I'm asking that every tear shed from this day forward would be tears of joy and not tears of sorrow. I bind any bitterness and hatred that she may hold in her heart, because we know these are things sent by the devil to distract us from you. God use Avery to be the source of strength in her home, give her the ability to weather this storm. Your word says that your strength is made perfect in our weakness, and at this moment Avery is weak and in need of your strength Father; and God we know that the only person that can take the pain away is you. So we are giving you everything tonight, from this point on what she sees and hear will not affect her faith but it will be made stronger. And God we love and we know these things are already done in your son Jesus name, Amen. Avery I don't know what's going on but I'm always a phone call away. Let God do what He has to do in this situation, we make it worse when we touch it ok?"

"You're right. How did you know that I needed you?" I asked as the prayer James just prayed for me resonated in my spirit. Since meeting him he has always been there for me even from hundreds of miles away.

I could hear him smile when he said, "I told you we are connected and no matter what I got you."

"Thanks James. I'll call you tomorrow and tell you all about it." I told him. Just that fast my tears had been dried and my frown was now replaced by a toothy smile.

"Ok. I'll be here. Love u Avey." He said. This wasn't the first time that he had said this but it was the first time I felt a spark in my heart when I heard it.

"I love you too." I said rushing off of the phone because I was unfamiliar with the feeling that I was feeling. One minute I was feeling proud as I put my sister to bed, then the next I was feeling rage watching my father with another woman, to now feeling butterflies in my stomach when my friend told me he loved me.

I was tripping now for real and knew that no studying would get done tonight. Just as I got under my covers and put my computer and books on the floor I heard that man come up the stairs. I couldn't even call him my father anymore because I didn't know who he was.

Pulling the covers over my head I left a little opening so that I could see my door but appear to be asleep. And just as I imagined he slowly opened my door to peek in and make sure I was asleep. I knew my room would be the one he checked because it was in the front of the house and he had to make sure he had gone unnoticed. Well little did he know that not only did God see him but I did too and in due time everyone one else would see him for who he really was. A no good snake in the grass that wore a collar and toted a bible.

It may not have been very Christian of me but every day since that night I prayed that just like God rained down burning sulfur onto the city of Sodom and Gomorrah that He would somehow do the same to Pastor Andrew Webber.

Chapter Seven

Jewel

I sat at my desk inside of my downstairs office and looked at the clock in the right hand bottom corner of my computer screen. The display showed the time as four in the afternoon and six days since Drew left to head to Atlanta. The time and date also reminded me that it had been six days since I last talked to him. If it wasn't me calling his phone it was Kammy trying to FaceTime him only to have the phone go straight to voicemail or just ring. As of nine this morning I had left so many messages that his mailbox was now filled to capacity.

I stopped making attempts to reach him the moment I logged into my personal Facebook page and saw that he had been posting and checking in at different locations in

Atlanta. At least he wasn't dead but once I reached him he was going to wish that he was.

Trying my best to take my mind off of what could possibly be going on with my husband I focused all of my energy and attention on the final details of his pastor's anniversary that would take place in four days. I was so excited for this new level that God was about to take us to but for some reason I didn't feel like Drew was taking it as seriously as I was. Maybe he was just nervous. This was a big step in ministry but I knew that he could handle it. Before I had the chance to get back to making sure everything was in order the house phone rang. Praying it was Drew finally calling I looked at the caller ID and saw it was my father.

"Hey my gem." He greeted me.

It seemed like he sensed when something was going on with me because he would always call at the right time.

"Hey Daddy. How are you? Where's mom?"

"Oh I'm fine. We just got back from one of her doctor's appointments." He said reminding me that she did have to go and get another mammogram done. Since the breast cancer that had claimed her left breast was in remission her doctor wanted to do regular mammograms and run test to make sure it hadn't returned.

My mother Francis was a trooper though. A real soldier for the Lord and no matter what went on with her she still gave God praise even in the darkest of times.

"That totally slipped my mind. What was the outcome?" I asked quickly saying a silent prayer that everything was still good.

I didn't realize I was holding my breath until I heard him say that everything was just fine and I was able to exhale. My mother was the reason that my father passed up being the head pastor of the church because he knew how much time was required when it came to ministry. His main focus was taking care of his family at home because if his home life was out of order there was no way that he could lead a church. I admired that about him, he really loved his family. I knew what it felt like to have such a positive man in my life growing up and what a husband should be, but there were days I felt like I didn't have that no matter how hard I tired ignoring the signs.

"I was calling baby girl to see how you are though. God has had you heavy on my heart and mind these last couple of days." He said.

I had gotten so caught up in my thoughts I forgot he was on the line.

"I'm ok. Just trying to make sure these last minute details are together before Drew gets back in time for the anniversary."

"Wait I thought Andrew was home already."

"No. Why would you think that Daddy? I told you he had a speaking engagement in Charlotte." I reminded him. He had me confused as to what he was talking about. I knew he wasn't losing his memory so the fact that he was thinking Drew was home and I had given him the schedule was beyond me.

"Doesn't Bryce go with him when he leaves town?" he asked me.

"Yes." I had no clue what he was getting at.

"Do they always come back together?"

"Yes. Daddy why are you asking me these questions?"

Now I was starting to worry again.

"I just saw Bryce at the grocery store. I stopped to talk to him for a few minutes about when he was going to finally decide to become a pastor. I see nothing but the hand of God on his life and I know he will be an awesome addition for the kingdom in that capacity. Unlike…." He trailed off.

My emotions were all over the place and I couldn't understand why Bryce was back and I didn't know where my husband was.

"Daddy I have to go. Tell mom I'll call her back later on and check on her. Love you." I said hanging up the phone not waiting on a response from him.

Something wasn't right and I began to wonder if the vision God gave to me the other night was about to come to pass. If so I was going to need all of His strength to get through this. Before I picked up the phone to call the hotel my husband should have been at and to check in with Bryce so that he could explain why he was home but Drew was MIA I reached in the top drawer of my desk and pulled out my bottle of Zoloft and popped two into my mouth. God in heaven knows if this didn't go right my next breakdown might send me over the deep end. The last time I slipped into a deep depression I was stuck in the bed for almost three weeks and if it hadn't been for Bryce coming to the house that day to see Drew my children would have been motherless. That man had really been there for a lot of the most difficult times in my life when my husband should have but none the less I was grateful for him.

Hopefully now he will have some answers for me that contradicted what my mind was already telling me.

Chapter Eight

Drew

Sitting behind the pulpit I look out into the faces of my congregation as they celebrated me. This was my church, my ministry, my flock. I run this show and have been for the last ten years so today on this Pastor's Anniversary I was going to sit back and watch as the people worshiped me. How could they not? If it wasn't for me half of these people would be jobless and without lights and food. They owed me so to speak. I looked over to the woman sitting beside me with the light make up, bouncy curls, and wide body and smiled. If I cared even a little bit about my wife I could say that God had truly blessed me with my Jewel. But I didn't. I was here for only one reason and that was to make a come up. Tomorrow morning would be the end of this charade I was putting on with both Jewel and Jasmine.

My wife and the mother of our two beautiful daughters, Jewel was some man's dream just not mine. My reality didn't include her for too much longer but I would act like it. She wasn't enough. I needed more. I chuckled to myself at that thought. Jewel was more than enough but I meant that literally.

Of course I heard the warnings daily from the Lord and even from my best friend Bryce but I was too smooth with mine. Unlike most men I was covered behind the cross. God may have warned me but He would never expose me. I preached His word to His people like He instructed and in return He kept my secrets covered.

I sat up in my seat and straightened my tie while the choir sang about His goodness. Yes He was good, very good, but I was a little better. I'm the epitome of a Man of

God on the outside but on the inside, that real life I live is what keeps me going. Something about this other life of mine keeps the fire burning in me. Yearning for more. The excitement of knowing my wife, children, and church will never know I pull the wool over their eyes daily gives me a since of power like no other.

I guess I owed a little thanks to Jewel for getting me here though. Had she not been about to receive some big inheritance there is no way I would be getting ready to head to take her for all she had. I could care less what she and the girls would be left with once I was gone because I'm sure I would be good for the rest of my life.

When the choir finally stopped singing and the people in the congregation got themselves together I stood to give my thanks as a feeling hit me like a ton of bricks. Another warning from God I suppose. "This is your last warning son." I heard but shook it off. He'll never expose me for who I really am, I'm His servant. I thought to myself. I looked over at Bryce and he had a look of satisfaction on his face. Not sure what that was about but I turned to my other side and as I bent down to kiss Jewel as I always did before preaching, instead of her kissing me back she turned her head to face the many faces of Living Testimony Christian Center.

Taken aback for just a quick second I gathered myself, smiled, and walked up to my podium. Right as I was opening my mouth to start my speech the doors of the church opened and I heard a voice that made me sick to my stomach.

"Good evening everyone. I'm Constance, the Preacher's other Woman."

Chapter Nine

Jewel

To say I was speechless would be an understatement. My whole body went numb as the revelation of my husband's infidelity hit me like a ton of bricks. I looked over to Bryce who wore the same shocked expression on his face that I had on mine. So many thoughts were going through my head yet nothing was forming to make sense at the moment.

I thought my heart had shattered when Bryce told me what Drew was up to but right now I felt like my heart was non-existent in my chest. God had allowed this man to snatch it right out of my body and I didn't understand why. I was a good wife and mother and tried to be the woman that Drew needed but it still wasn't enough.

"Good evening everyone." The woman named Constance said again.

"Babe what are you doing here?" Drew said clearing his throat.

You could hear a pin drop the church was so quiet.

"Drew what's going on?" I asked finally finding my voice but I couldn't stop it from shaking.

"Shut up Jewel. Answer the question Constance." He said not even looking at me.

"NO!" I said letting them all know I was not playing this time.

"What's going on honey is I'm tired of not being able to have my man home with me and our children on a regular basis." Constance informed me.

There was no way I could keep the tears from flowing no matter how hard I tried. Looking at this woman stand in front of me made me sick to my stomach. She was gorgeous. I knew her hair wasn't real but the long blond weave was freshly curled and fell around her caramel colored face. Her eyes were dark and slanted almost like if you wore a ponytail too tight and it caused your eyes to be stretched. As bad as I didn't want to look at her body I couldn't help it. The woman was flawless compared to me. She wasn't real tall but she was taller than me and her weight complimented her frame well. Constance was everything I wasn't and thoughts of Romeo came flooding back to my memory.

Without a second thought the embarrassment I felt carried me down the stairs of the stage and out of the side door leading to my office. I had to get out of there and I needed to fast. If I didn't the rage inside of me would have taken over at that moment. Although I wanted my husband to come behind me to make sure I was ok and to let me know that this was all just a misunderstanding, I knew that wasn't going to happen.

Drew looked at her with so much love in his eyes. Love that in the last eighteen years I've known him I'd never once seen. That's when it hit me. Andrew Webber did not marry me because he loved me. He married me because he wanted what I had to offer. Bryce had already filled me in on what was going on but I didn't want to believe him. I had no choice now. The truth just walked in and stared me in my face so there was no denying it.

I heard the door to Drew's office slam shut and was immediately followed by arguing.

"God give me comfort because if you give me strength to handle this situation I'm using it and I'm going to jail," I said out loud.

Before I could reach the doorknob on the adjoining door that led to the Pastor's Study my main office door opened and Bryce came in.

"J just go home. Let me handle this for you." He said.

Instead of listening to him or responding I opened the door and walked through it.

******

"I told you that if you didn't leave her I was going to make sure she did myself!"

"You had no right! I told you that I was going to leave once everything was final."

"So this was planned Drew?" I asked startling them both.

"What do you think Sherlock?" Constance said to me. The beautiful woman I had just seen ten minutes prior was now so ugly to me.

"Man. Go on Jewel. I'm talking to my fiancé." He said without a hint of remorse.

Red. That's exactly all I saw right now and as I charged at the both of them I felt Bryce grab me from behind to stop me.

"I hope you ate your Wheaties this morning bro cause that's a big one you holding back." Drew said laughing.

"How could you say and do something like this yo?" Bryce asked him as I continued to cry.

Before Drew could answer the main door to his office opened up and in walked Jasmine.

"Yea how could you do this Drew?" she asked walking further into the room with my three year old God son in tow.

I felt the grip Bryce had around my waist get tighter and I wondered why. And what was Jasmine doing here anyway. When I invited her to the anniversary she told me that she couldn't make it because her son DJ was sick.

"Jaz what are you doing here?" I asked. Instead of her answering me she kept her eyes trained on Drew. That was when it hit me like a ton of bricks. Jasmine wasn't asking why he did this to me. She was asking why he was doing this to *her*.

"Who are you?" Constance asked. Looking from Drew to Jasmine.

"I'm the mother of his child." She simply replied.

"Oh God no." I said as I felt like the air in the room was slowly being sucked out.

Chapter Ten

Drew

This could not be life right now. This was not the way that this was supposed to be happening. This time tomorrow I should be on a plane to an island somewhere with Constance. I knew that last warning that God sent me I should have taken heed to but I couldn't walk away until I got what was owed to me. I deserved whatever it was that Jewel was getting from her grandfather just for dealing with her all of these years. She definitely owed me.

"What are you doing here?" I asked Jasmine completely ignoring everyone else's questions.

"Don't play dumb now. I told you that I was tired of waiting on you to leave her." She said tilting her head in the direction of Jewel. Bryce still had a hold on her and I know he was getting tired because she wouldn't keep still. That was a lot to hold on to.

"Come on you know I told you I don't know how many times that I wasn't going to settle down with you. Even after you had my son you knew that wouldn't change my feelings for you. You were just a means to an end for me." I finally told her the truth.

I was tired of playing these games with these women. It was time that I put it all out there what was going on.

"Ok. Everybody want to know the truth then here it is." I said prepared to take them back down memory lane.

****

I was chopping it up at a frat party when in walked Jasmine and Jewel. Jasmine and I had already been fooling around for some time when she mentioned to me one night how much she disliked her roommate. She went into detail about how good Jewel had it but how she was always complaining. Jewels' self-esteem was so low and it made no sense to her. She would do anything to live the life that Jewel was.

As soon as she started telling me about how Jewel would get an inheritance once she got married the wheels in my head started turning. She was so focused on venting that she didn't even know that I was fishing for info from her. Pillow talk could be a gift and a curse in a relationship.

"What kind of inheritance?" I asked as I began to caress her thighs while we sat on the couch in my dorm. I

knew it wouldn't take much to get the information from her. She couldn't hold water in a cup.

"Her grandfather left her father, her, and her brother some money when he died but there were stipulations in place and if they didn't meet them they couldn't get the money." She said.

"Stipulations?"

"Yeah. She had to graduate at the top of her class and get married in order to receive it."

"How much is it?" I pried.

"Now that I don't know. She keeps hush mouth about that but it has to be a lot. She said he had money because of all of the businesses he owned and the church that he started from the ground up."

"But I thought yall were cool." I said just to see where her mind was about Jewel. If my gut was right her answer would confirm it to me.

"Boy bye! I only hang around her cause when her parents do for her they do for me. And if I play my cards right when she gets her money she won't have a problem sharing. Besides I'm the only friend she has."

That night Jasmine and I came up with an air tight plan to get that money by any means necessary and the night of the party was just the beginning.

"So you plotted against me?" Jewel asked bring me back from my thoughts.

"Girl don't act like you didn't know something was up. Look at you. You're fat and you dressed like an old woman. Why would he want something like you on his arm unless you had something that he wanted?" Jasmine scoffed.

"She has a point there. Under normal circumstances you wouldn't have gotten the time of day from me but all I saw was dollar signs." I said pouring salt on Jewel's open wounds.

"Where do you fit in?" Jewel turned to Constance and asked her. I had almost forgotten she was there because she had been so quiet.

"I don't know. Where do I fit in Drew?" she asked me.

Without a word I walked over to her pulling her in close to me and giving her the deepest most passionate kiss I had ever given her. Next thing I know Jasmine had let go of my son's hand and was landing blow after blow on Constance. It took her a minute to get her bearings together from being caught off guard but once she did it was over for Jasmine.

It took me at least two minutes to pry Constance's hands from Jasmine's hair and to stop the blows that were landing each and every time. My son DJ was yelling at the top of his lungs from all of the commotion and trying to grab my leg.

"Bryce man help me!" I yelled needing him to help me get this situation under control but I was still struggling.

"BRYCE!" I called out again. When I still didn't get a response I turned around to see Bryce and Jewel were no longer in the room but my two daughters were with tears in their eyes. It caused me to pause for a brief moment as I looked into their innocent faces but I didn't feel any remorse at all.

"I hate you so much!" Avery screamed as she grabbed Kammy's hand and ran out of the room.

I turned back around to face the other two women in my life who I could tell were finally getting tired of fighting.

"Yall done?" I asked with a smirk on my face as they both parted and stood on each side of the room.

"Choose." Was all Jasmine said.

Without another word I walked over to her as a smile began to spread across her face. I could tell she thought she had come out on top but that smile would soon fade with my next few words.

"You're dead to me." I said with each syllable laced with ice.

"What about DJ? All of these years together and you are just going to leave us?" she cried.

I didn't bother to even respond as I grabbed Constance's hand and headed to the front of the church. As soon as I rounded the corner leading to the outside I was surprised to see so many people still there. I guess I shouldn't have been because people loved it when a scandal jumped off no matter where it happened but the church poured the best tea I guess. I knew by the look on their faces that they expected me to be running behind Jewel and our daughters or giving some kind of explanation of what was going on but I owed no one a thing. So I kept my head up as I cockily walked out with Constance in tow.

"Pastor! Pastor Webber!" I heard Mother Johnson call out to me right before I got to my 2015 Mercedes S550. I had just bought this car the other day with the rest of the money I had in my separate account that Jewel didn't know anything about. It didn't matter to me that I had spent those few dollars. Little did my wife know I had found the necessary documents that I needed in order to change the account info for the inheritance deposit that would deposit tonight at midnight. I was about to be a millionaire and it was way overdue. Tomorrow Constance, our two children, and myself would be high in the air on the way to our new life in Aruba.

"Yes Mother?" I said not trying to hide the fact that I was annoyed and ready to go.

"Why are you doing this son? This isn't right and God is not pleased." She said with tears in her eyes.

"And what am I doing Mother Johnson?" I asked folding my arms across my chest.

"All of this! Cheating on your wife with all of these lowlife women and fathering all of these children behind her back. What true man of God would carry on like this?" clearly she was upset but it didn't move me but I bet what I said next moved her.

"I don't know what kind of man would do his wife like this. Why don't you ask Deacon Johnson and Sister Thelma?"

Checkmate. I thought as I watched the color drain from Mother Johnson's light skinned face. I turned away from her and unlocked the door to get in the car but before I could close the door she had one last thing to say to me.

"God says, 'Vengeance is Mine, and retribution. In due time their foot will slip. For the day of their calamity is near and the impending things are hastening upon them.' Your day is coming and when it does you and everyone you are connected to will pay." She said walking off.

"Her husband really messing around?" Constance asked me.

"Nah but it was funny to see her reaction. She gonna give that old man hell when she gets home?" I told her as we fell out laughing and speeding out of the parking lot.

Chapter Eleven

Bryce

I swear I needed God to step in and intervene on Jewels behalf. I hated seeing her in this condition and all over a man that meant her no good. I knew I probably should have just kept my mouth shut and none of this would have even happened but when I sat back and thought about it I remembered that this wasn't my fault. I wasn't the one that was married with children and living a secret life Drew was and he was causing nothing but pain to the ones he should have been protecting and loving. Jewel was an amazing woman and she didn't deserve to be treated like this. So I felt it was finally time that she knew everything and I told her. I just had no idea that all of this other stuff was going on too.

Drew never made it a secret that there were many women in his life. I mean we both did. We were young and not committed to anyone but once he finally got with Jewel and I met her I immediately told him to stop playing games. There was something about her that I never saw in any of the women either of us dealt with. Jewel was the epitome of that blessed woman that was talked about in Proverbs 31. Her worth was undeniably worth more than those rubies and though many women do noble things she surpasses them all. Too bad Drew missed the most important things about her but I didn't. I just didn't know how to step to her because from the beginning her eyes were on him. So I fell back but not too far. Every chance I got I was telling Drew to either let her go or treat her right but he just didn't listen. I wish I had gone harder for her back then and maybe I could have protected the hearts of her and those girls. It was too late now though so I had to figure out what to do to mend the pieces back together for them all.

I pulled up in my parent's driveway because I seriously needed to talk to my dad. Unlike so many men these days my father had always been very active in my life. Growing up I watched as he sacrificed so much for our family to make sure that we were well taken care of. Not only was he a very good provider but he also made sure we had strong relationships with God. From as far back as I can remember we were in church learning about the Son of God and how He died for all of our sins. It took me so long to understand why someone would lay down their life for me just so that I could have eternal life. I would always say I'm not dying for anyone but my parents but once I met Jewel that all changed.

Yes I grew up knowing that what I was doing with these women wasn't right but temptation is a beast. Once I got started it was like a high chasing them. I kept looking for the next woman to come along and top that last high but they all fell short and when I met Jewel. I knew then that the reason I couldn't find the feeling I was seeking was because everything I needed and wanted was planted in her. The revelation of when a man finds a wife he finds a good thing was clear as day for me. But I was too late getting to her. Drew beat me to the punch and by then he had her wrapped around his finger.

Knowing Drew the way I did I knew he wasn't really into her and once he told me the reason he was with her I lost it. He thought that I was upset because I wasn't able to get to her for her inheritance but the truth was I was upset because I knew her heart would end up broken. I wanted so bad to keep her heart intact because she didn't deserve to be hurt like that.

Drew had told me everything about how insecure she was and how that was his way in. I tried so many times to make him see what he was doing to her but he didn't care. The dollar signs were clouding his vision and causing him not to care about anyone but Andrew.

After sitting a few minutes in the driveway getting my thoughts together I finally turned off the car and headed up the steps to their front door. I prayed my dad wasn't asleep because it was a little after nine at night but I couldn't sleep knowing that Jewel and those girls were at home in pain. I opened the door with my key and headed into the foyer. The light to my father's office was on and I could see it illuminating under the closed door.

"Come on in son." I heard him say to me.

I opened the door and saw my father sitting behind his large oak desk with his glasses on and a notepad in front of him. From the looks of things he was preparing a message that he would have to soon deliver a word to God's people in the absence of their beloved leader.

"How did you know it was me?" I asked taking a seat in front of him and propping my foot up on my knee.

"Well it would sound real good if I said that the Lord told me you were coming but since I'm not gonna lie on Him like that, I saw you coming from the kitchen window." He said in his deep baritone voice while he chuckled lightly.

Although my father was going on a cool seventy years old he didn't look a day over forty. He stood a firm six foot two with salt and pepper hair and dark brown skin. He seemed to always have a twinkle in his eyes and he kept his body fit. I understood why my mother was always all over him even in their old age. Pops was that dude and everyone always told me I was his twin.

"So what brings you by this late son?" he wanted to know.

I took a deep breath and exhaled before I began to let my father in on my feelings.

"Pop I'm in love." I said not sure if I wanted to look him in his face because what I was about to say would surely be frowned upon.

"Oh yeah?" was all he said taking his glasses off and sitting back in his high back chair.

"Yeah but I know it will never work."

"Why is that?" he asked.

"She's married and already has children." I said. I thought I would be ashamed once I said it out loud but surprisingly I wasn't. It had actually felt good and like a weight was taken off of my shoulder.

"Does she now?" he was starting to frustrate me. I just wanted him to go ahead and tell me something to help me understand all that I was feeling.

"Dad I don't know what to do." I said getting up and walking to the back of the room.

"Have you told Jewel how you feel yet?" he asked causing me to spin around so fast I almost fell.

"Wait. How do you know that's who I'm talking about?" I couldn't remember a time where I had done anything inappropriate around or to her so I was lost at how he knew.

"Your eyes." Was his simple response.

I'm sure the confusion was displayed all over the place but I couldn't help it. I was dumfounded.

"You know how everyone says that we look so much alike?"

I simply nodded my head and wondered what that had to do with anything. He must have known that's what I was thinking because he started to explain himself.

"I remember the first weekend you came home after going off to college and you told us that you think your found your wife?" he said bringing back the memory.

I didn't realize I was smiling at the thought until he said,

"That same smile you have right now is the same one you had when you told us about her and the same look I had when I met your mother. When I set eyes on my good thing I knew she was the one. That's how your mother and I knew Jewel was the one for you."

"Mom knows?"

"Of course. She's always wanted the two of you together."

"But she's married and that goes against God." I said to him.

"Has that stopped you before?" my mother said coming into the room and startling me. She kissed me on my head and went over to sit on my father's lap.

There was that look that he was talking about. It's crazy because that's the same way that I admire Jewel but from a distance. But I didn't know what she was getting at. I knew personally what she meant but I had no clue how she found out. I had been so careful.

"Ma what do you mean has that stopped me before?" God knows I prayed for forgiveness.

She dropped her head to the side like that dude Foxy who waits for people at "da doe".

"Just what I said. It hasn't stopped you before so why are you letting it stop you now when clearly this is meant to be."

"I'm still lost."

"Baby Ray Charles, Stevie Wonder, and the Three Blind Mice can all see that Kammy is your daughter. You, Jewel, and Andrew seem to be the only ones that don't see it. Or maybe you all are in denial." She said bursting my bubble.

It never crossed my mind that anyone would see the resemblance between me and Kam. The whole nine months Jewel carried her I was a nervous wreck. I didn't know if she was going to look just like me or if she would look like Drew. I just knew that we couldn't hold that secret for long but once she entered the world and I saw how Drew seemed to fall in love with my daughter I backed off.

Maybe that was the reason that I couldn't hold in what Drew was doing behind her back. I wanted to be able to raise my daughter and be with the woman I loved.

"Baby listen." My mother said coming over to sit beside me as she took my hand in hers.

"You can't help who it is that you fall in love with and although you and Jewel made a mistake I'm pretty sure the both of you have repented and asked God for forgiveness. He has already done that now it's time for you to move forward. Jewel doesn't deserve to be treated the way that she is and neither does those girls but now it's time for you to help pick up the pieces and mend their broken hearts.

I'm not saying go over there right now and woo her and jump in her bed once again but what I'm saying is be there for that woman. You know that news travels mighty fast around here so I already know what happened at that church earlier. The last thing she needs is to feel that you are just there because you pity her but I honestly feel like she married the wrong man and he took advantage of her already brokenness and used it to his advantage. Remember though that God still sits high and looks low so you better believe Drew will get what's coming to him.

She needs you son. Just pray and ask God to guide you during this time. There may be a piece of paper that says she is married to Drew but that is the only thing that connects them. You are connected to her heart and her spirit." And with that she stood up and kissed me on my cheek.

"Thanks Ma and Pops. I love you."

"I love you too baby. Now get out. Your father and I have things to tend to if you know what I mean." She said winking at my dad.

"Eeww yall nasty."

"Yep. Just the way I like it." My dad said standing and moving towards my mother.

"I'm out!" I said moving as fast as I could to the front door as they laughed.

Chapter Twelve

Jewel

All I could do was sit in our driveway and cry for hours and hours. Not one of those ugly cries that women do when the pain is fresh and unexpected. I mean one of those silent cries. The ones where your mind couldn't process the betrayal or hurt that was so deep in your being. The one that you cried when you already expected the pain to hit but didn't know that it could hurt as bad as it did. Where the only two functions that your body could remember to do was to breathe and let the tears fall. You feel nothing but emptiness and just wanting out. Wanting out of the emotional bondage but feeling like in some crazy way you needed that bondage in order to survive.

When you didn't want to hear someone say, "God is still in control. Just let Him have His way." Instead you wanted to hear them tell you that it was ok to be mad at God because He let this happen. And scream and curse everybody out who tells you that everything will be just fine.

Everything would not be just fine. The man that I gave my heart and innocence to had gone back on the promises he made to me in front of God and our loved ones. He had something that no other man had ever gotten. Something so precious that should have been handled with care but instead was thrown away like last week's garbage.

As selfish as it sounded I just wanted God to take me away from this misery and this hell I was living on earth. At this very moment I understood why people gave up when everything they worked so hard for came crashing down around them. I was broken and my being couldn't take any more of the disappointments.

I had sat in this car so long that it was now dark outside. Avery kept peeking her head out of the door and window every thirty minutes or so checking on me. I could only imagine what was going through my children's minds right now but I didn't have anything comforting to say to them. It may have been selfish of me but I honestly couldn't form any reasonable explanation to give them nor did I want to.

Looking over at the fluorescent numbers on my radio display showed me that I had been sitting in my car for the last four hours and I didn't plan on getting out anytime soon. I honestly wanted to drive until my eyes got heavy and sleep consumed me and then death took over but I knew that would be unfair to the girls. Their father had already taken so much from them and I wasn't going to add to that. I had to find a way to get past this so that I could be there for them. They were really all that I had left and the only positive outcome to this madness.

I sat back and thought about when I placed that call to the hotel a few days ago and found out that my husband had canceled his reservations unlike the lie he told me about it being sold out. Digging further into things I discovered he wasn't in Charlotte like he told us but he was actually in Atlanta. The Facebook posts that he was making and checking in at were just to throw me off but it wouldn't be for long. I may have been quiet and had issues with my physical appearance but I was as smart as they come. Never did I think would I have to go snooping behind my husband but in the event that I did there was nothing that man could hide from me, on paper that is. Drew was definitely clever because although I found out about the other women, and even Constance, I never once knew about Jewel. He covered his tracks very well with that one.

Something told me a long time ago I shouldn't trust Jewel but I put my heart before what I felt in my spirit. Being in a new area away from family and already having a hard time adjusting, I just wanted to enjoy the college experience with a true friend. So I put all of the negative thoughts about her being a "wolf in sheep's clothing" out of my mind. God had given me signs time after time about her but I always blocked them out. That's something so many people do when they know in their hearts that He is trying to lead us right but our flesh a lot of times want what the flesh wants and we choose to ignore it. To think of how much heartache I could have prevented for myself and our daughters if I had just completely surrendered myself to what I was hearing.

Our daughters. I thought to myself but before I could dwell on that too long I looked up to see a car pulling up beside me in Drew's space in the driveway. I knew it wasn't him before I could even see the car clearly. When I heard how he called Constance his "babe" and how he looked at her so lovingly that was the defining moment is our marriage that it was over. I felt and saw the love he had for her and even after almost twenty years together I had never felt that from him. God knows I yearned for it and I stayed praying he would give it to me but it never came. Well not from him anyway.

I watched as Bryce got out of his car and stood there looking at me through the window. The look on his face let me know that he had been crying and his heart was hurting for me. No words were spoken as I hit the unlock button and he reached his hand out to open my door. Neither of us moved nor did we break the intense gaze between us. The way this man looked at me was the same way that I desired the man that I had married to look at me. The power and intensity seemed to transfer from him to me and there was no denying the presence of God that was resonating between us.

Without a single word he just opened his arms and at the same time a tear made its way down his right cheek. Before I could really process what was happening I ended up in his arms releasing every ounce of pain, hurt, and neglect that I had been holding on to all of these years. Feeling like I was in a safe place I finally cried my ugly cry.

Chapter Thirteen

Jasmine

I couldn't believe this was happening as I sat on the bed in my hotel room. All of these years Drew had been playing me and making me think that it was all about me and our son but it was all lies. I should have figured out after the first few years something wasn't right but I let my heart lead me instead of listening to my grandmother when she kept saying to me the same way you get a man is the same way that you could lose him. But I was hardhead and wanted what I wanted.

Looking over at my three year old son I thought back to when I first told Drew I was pregnant with DJ. This wasn't my first pregnancy by him but this was definitely the one I was going to keep. I was tired of killing all of my babies for this man just because he kept telling me to wait until he moved on from Jewel. We had been together for over ten years by then and I wanted to have a family with him. What I didn't expect was that he had another family that neither Jewel nor I knew about.

True Jewel had the right to be hurt because she was the one that he actually married but I had a right too because I was with him first. If anyone should have been on top it was me. I held him down like no other and if it wasn't for me he would have never known about the inheritance. Andrew Webber owed me my part of the money and bright and early I was going to be at that meeting he thought I didn't know anything about. He thought that he was so slick and that he could trust me not to snoop through his stuff but what he didn't realize that no matter how loyal a woman was to her man there was always something to let her know when something wasn't right and we would go digging.

Before he had come to visit this last time I knew that it was now or never that I found out all that I could. Each time I brought the subject up previously about how much we were getting he would change the subject like I was stupid. It had to be a grip because he was too hush hush for me now days. In the beginning he was very open about what was going on and even told me the things he needed me to do on my end. This was all supposed to benefit not just him but for our family that he wanted to be with. Nothing but lies and I fell for it hook, line, and sinker.

I should have known things were off when he didn't leave at the five year mark like he initially planned. Something about it not looking right if he left right after they received the money but that was all another lie. During my search in his email I found the documents that stated he had to remain married to Jewel, have children, and be in the lead pastor position at her family's church for ten years. After the tenth year Pastor's Anniversary ceremony they were to inherit a cool twenty million dollars. Constantly telling me that he only had to be there only a little while and we would be set but he knew all along that wasn't the case.

It finally hit me that he was planning on leaving with all of that money and living with his other family. He was not about to walk off into the sunset with another woman and kids along with all of that money. My son and I were going to be set weather he liked it or not or like my boy Plies said, "It's goin down tonight cause these goons out lurkin!"

Chapter Fourteen

Drew

Laying in the king size bed at the Hilton in Augusta I couldn't contain the excitement that I was feeling. In less than thirty minutes I would be logging into my online account and seeing so many zeros it would make my head swim and I couldn't wait to get on with my life. I can't say that the life I lived so far wasn't good but it just wasn't with the person that I wanted it to be with. Not saying that I wanted it to go down like it did at the church earlier but I couldn't blame Constance for wanting this to all be over.

She had been my rider ever since I met her a year after marrying Jewel and unlike Jasmine, Constance didn't need me for anything. Jewel constantly needed me to validate her and make her feel beautiful and I just didn't have that in me. Then there was Jasmine that wanted me to take care of her and her material needs. Constance on the other hand needed me for nothing. She had her own home, paid her own bills, took wonderful care of our kids, and was the woman that I needed in and out of the bedroom.

"So why haven't you let that lil bust down Jasmine go yet?" Constance asked me coming out of the bathroom.

Everything about her was beautiful to me. From her long straight weave that she kept done to the caramel skin that covered her slim toned body. Her eyes were slightly slanted like a cat and her pearly white smile could light up any room.

"Come on now babe. You know that was just to make all of this look good." I said getting up and walking over to her as she began to lotion her body.

I took the bottle out of her hand and began to let the anointing flow through my fingers as I caressed her body. Constance tilted her head to the side and let out a soft moan. Every time she made that sound it turned me on like no other and it became hard to focus as the blood rushed down below. Turning her around to face me, I put her arms around my neck and pulled her in closer as my mouth met hers and our lips began to worship one another.

Constance broke our kiss but not our stare as she walked backwards over to the bed and eased back on it. The look on her face was the sexiest thing I had ever seen at that moment and while I should have been able to block out every other thought while I looked at her I couldn't help thinking about Jewel. As long as we were married she would never let me look at her naked body in the light, not that I really wanted to, but it was the principle of the matter.

Not sure what made me look at the clock but I looked over on the nightstand and it read a half past midnight but I didn't remember getting a notification from my bank app like I usually did when I got a deposit. That was odd and although Constance was waiting on me in all of her naked glory that would have to wait. I needed to see what was going on with my money.

"What are you doing?" she asked me with a look of disappointment on her face.

"It's after midnight and I don't remember getting a notification of the deposit. Maybe with all of your moaning I couldn't hear it." I said with a smirk on my face.

"Well hurry up because I don't know how much longer I can wait. You do know that it's been over a month since I have been able to feel your touch.

"Trust me I know. And just as soon as I finish this I'm going to show you something else that I know well."

I went over to pick up my cell phone and noticed that I hadn't had one missed call from Jewel. To say I was shocked would be an understatement considering that she was always blowing my phone up. Before I went to my online bank app I did see that I had a text from my daughter.

Avery: I hope it was all worth it. Remember you reap what you sow. No matter if it's a good harvest or a bad one but you will reap it. I'm just glad that you are finally out of our lives and my mother can be with someone who will appreciate and love her unconditionally. I pray God has mercy on your soul.

There was no need to respond to her because she had no clue how covered I was. I preached the word of God better than any preacher, pastor, reverend, or bishop that I knew and there was no way God was going to pour out a cup of wrath on me. I could have looked at the situation at church as Him outing me but in actuality He helped me.

After I deleted the text message I blocked both Avery and Jewel's numbers. I didn't need either of them having access to me after tonight. I opened my Bank of America app and saw that my account was still showing a balance of -$5,263.89. Before I began to panic I noticed my email icon in the top left hand corner of my phone and clicked on it. The first few emails were just random stuff but what caught my attention was the one with the subject *"Rivers Family Inheritance Documents"*.

I noticed that the email wasn't highlighted like it was a new but like it had already been read. It was dated a week ago while I was in Atlanta with Jasmine but for the life of me I didn't remember reading it. To think about it that week was really a blur because all I did was stay in the bed with Jasmine. I knew it was about to be over and although I wasn't in love with her I was in love with what her body could do to mine. The second I opened it my heart sank to my feet.

"Oh sh-" I started but cut it off because I couldn't believe what I was reading.

"Drewsey what's wrong?" Constance asked sounding concerned as I could feel her moving behind me and leaning over my shoulder to see what had gotten me tongue tied.

Dear Pastor Webber,

My name is Brian Andrews and I am the attorney for the Rivers family. It has come to my attention that there was a change in the original bank account information that was initially verified by both your wife Jewel Rivers Webber and yourself. Upon further inspection I noticed that Mrs. Webber signed the documents but you did not. In order to make the transaction complete I would

need for you to come into my office no later than November

25, 2014. Once you have completed the signing of all

documents the transfer will be complete.

I'm apologize for any inconvenience this may have

caused. If you have any questions or cannot make it to my

office please give me a call. Listed below is the number

where you can reach me as well as my office address and

hours of availability.

Have a good afternoon,

Brian Andrews Attorney at Law

Once Constance finished reading I was already

pacing the floor. I didn't know what to do and all of my

plans seemed to be falling apart. This time tomorrow I

should have been on an island with the love of my life and

our kids but now I had to push my departure back.

"Babe stop pacing you're making me nervous."

"You're nervous?" I said with an obvious attitude.

"Uh yeah. Why shouldn't I be? You are the one walking around here looking like a mad man." She said turning her back to me.

Before I knew what was happening or was able to control myself I had yoked Constance up by her throat and had her pinned against the wall. This was a side of me that no one knew but Jasmine. I stayed having to put my hands on her because her mouth was so slick but Constance never gave me that problem. That was until today.

For some reason the pressure of getting outed at church, my daughter Avery trying to put her mouth on a man of God, and not getting my money as planned caused me to snap.

"Don't you ever in your life turn your back on me when I'm talking to you. Do you understand me?" I asked through gritted teeth.

To my surprise the look in her eyes held no fear. It was actually kind of sexy to me when I thought about it. But what she said next changed all of that for me.

"You better gone and kill me now because if you ever put your hands on me again I will slit your throat and cry at your funeral like a grieving widow. Now let me go."

The iciness of her tone and the fire in her eyes caused me to do just what she had commanded. I stepped back and watched her walk over to the bed and get right back in the same position she was in before I read that email. There was fire still in her eyes but the fire of anger was now replaced by the fire of lust. Her body was now the one giving out commands and just like a few minutes

before I obliged.

Chapter Fifteen

Bryce

Once I left my parent's house all I could do was drive around with no destination in sight. I didn't want to go home and be alone with my thoughts so driving around with my worship music on low and talking to God was what I needed. The more I talked to Him the more I felt that I was finally understanding my purpose and where I needed to be.

Not everyone would understand what was going on but I knew that God worked in mysterious ways and this was all His doing. As much as it hurt Jewel to find out this way she was stronger than she gave herself credit for. Her inner strength to me was just as sexy as her outer appearance and I knew it was just the way God had built her. She may have thought it would take her a long time to get over this but I doubted it. I prayed and prayed that the pain she felt would not last long for her or the girls and that if it was God's will He would allow me to be what they all needed.

As crazy as all of this sounded or will look to so many people I knew that this was what God had for my life. There are so many times we take situations into our own hands when we can clearly hear the voice of our Father in heaven directing us to go one way but what's presented to our flesh looks like the better choice. We mess ourselves up and have to deal with a season, sometimes a few seasons, of darkness that may take us years to be able to see the light again.

Me not going for what I knew God presented to me in Jewel all of those years ago caused me to miss out on so much. It caused her to deal with pain and disappointment for so long. It also caused me not to be there for my children. Yes that's plural. Both Kammy *and* Avery were my daughters but it seemed that no one picked up on that. My parents could tell Kam was my child because she looked just like me and although Avery resembled me some she was the spitting image of her mother.

Neither Jewel nor myself was proud of the mistakes we had made not once but twice but it was time to finally face the music. On the two occasions that our emotions and hormones got out of control Jewel conceived our daughters. Like I said before God works in mysterious ways and we won't always understand them.

My mind was so focused on what I was going to do I hadn't even realized that I had made it to Jewel's house until I pulled into the driveway. I noticed the living room light was on as well as the light in Avery's room since she faced the front of the house. Just as I was about to back out of the driveway because I didn't want to disturb them I looked to my left and saw Jewel sitting in her car crying.

As soon as our eyes met I knew that she was in need. I could tell by the look on her face that she was kind of hoping it was Drew coming home but her eyes also revealed that she was glad it was me,

I got out of my car all the while keeping my eyes on her. Neither of us broke the stare as I got closer to her. Without a word she unlocked the door and I wasted no time opening it for her. The love that I had for her by now was so overwhelming and powerful that I couldn't keep the tears from falling from my eyes as I opened my arms to receive her in them. I prayed that she wouldn't make me feel like a fool and shun me but to my relief she got out and fell right into me. Holding her in my arms was one of the best feelings in the world and though we were both hurting I wouldn't change this moment for anything in the world.

******

It felt like hours that we had been standing outside crying in one another's arms before we actually got ourselves together and went inside. Walking through the foyer this time felt nothing like any of the other times before this. Usually when I came over I felt a weight so heavy every time I walked inside but tonight that burden was nowhere to be found.

Making it into the house I continued to hold Jewel as she cried on my shoulder. I couldn't imagine the hurt and pain that she was feeling right now. Just by the look on her face I knew the hurt was deep and it was breaking me down that I couldn't do a thing right now but pray for her.

Once she was seated in the living room I went to the guest bathroom to get her some tissue and a warm rag for her face. Before I took it to her I went into the kitchen and got her a glass of ice water to drink. Moving about this house felt like I was right at home and although I shouldn't have been thinking about that at a time like this I couldn't help but to take notice of it.

Walking back into the room I saw Avery sitting there with her head on her mother's shoulder as Kammy sat on her other side wiping Jewel's tears away. It was at this moment that I knew that I had to be there for the three of them come hell or high water. No matter what I would not let them down and I would help build them back up as long as God allowed me to.

"Here sweetheart take this." I said handing the items to Jewel. She looked up and me and smiled but said not a word. I sat down on the other couch and just observed the three women that sat before me.

Avery was growing into a wonderful young woman. She was smart, focused, and on the way to much success in her life. She was one of the few young girls at our church that really put God first in everything that she did and I could only thank Jewel for instilling that into her.

Kammy was such a sweet little girl. So innocent and inquisitive but she brought pure joy into the lives of everyone that she came in contact with. But the look that they each had on their faces right now tore me to pieces. The one man that was supposed to constantly love and protect them had hurt each one of them in the worst possible way. But as long as I had breath in my body I wouldn't dare allow anyone to hurt them ever again. If it took the rest of my life to make them feel better and to take the hurt away, I would do it until God called me home.

Chapter Sixteen

Avery

I heard my mother come in the house and I knew she wasn't alone. I had watched from my bedroom window as my father drove up in his car, opened her door, and she fell into the arms of the man that God had had for her. Yes I knew that Bryce was my biological father. I had known for a few weeks now and I was actually excited about it. Neither him nor my mother knew that I had found out and I wanted to wait for them to tell me first, but with everything going on I felt like maybe I should bring it up to ease their minds.

"Um I need to talk to you two about something. I know that this may not be the best time but then again maybe this is the perfect time." I said to them. I watched as my mother wiped her tears and gave me her undivided attention. This was another reason that I loved her so much. No matter what she was feeling or going through she made sure to make my sister and I her priority if we needed her.

"What is it baby?" She asked me.

"I need to talk to you about something I heard a few weeks ago. I didn't mean to eavesdrop but when I heard you on the phone that day Mommy I couldn't help it." I said as I dropped my head.

"Hold your head up sweetie. There is no need to be ashamed. What did you hear?"

Instead of just blurting out what I heard I went back to that day from the beginning.

Three Weeks Ago

I had gotten home earlier than normal because it was an early release day for the seniors at school. I was shocked to see my mom's car in the driveway because usually she got home after Kammy and I did on Thursdays. She had so much work to do at the church to get ready for the upcoming Pastor's Anniversary and had been working overtime. But she wasn't alone. My grandparent's car was there as well.

Walking into the house I could hear the faint voices coming from her office on the other side of the kitchen. As I got closer to the door I saw that it was slightly opened and it sounded like I heard my mother crying. I didn't know what was going on and I didn't want to barge in if they were talking about something important. As I turned around to head up to my room I heard my grandfather say something that stopped me dead in my tracks.

"Well if you ask me I'm glad that Bryce is the father of the girls."

Wait what? What girls was he referring to?

I couldn't move my feet even if I wanted to. It was as if they were now planted in a bucket of cement. Was my grandfather saying that Uncle Bryce was the father of both my sister and I instead of Drew?

"But it wasn't supposed to be like this Daddy. I have sinned against God and committed adultery against my husband. There is no way that I could be forgiven for this. It's frowned upon." I heard my mother say.

This explained so much to me at that moment. I had always had a deeper connection with Uncle Bryce than I did with my father. I couldn't stand that man. I always knew that something wasn't right with him. I never felt that father daughter connection that I heard girls talk about that they shared with their fathers. Even the relationship that my mom and grandfather had was special. Drew and I never shared that. And after that night I caught him come home with that woman anything that I did feel for him was dead that night.

"Listen sweetie," my grandmother started, 'Everything happens for a reason. Now I don't condone stepping outside of your marriage but I also understand that you were vulnerable and being mistreated. Drew never really loved you like he should and no one was able to open your eyes but Bryce. I honestly prayed that you didn't marry Andrew and instead marry Bryce but your father told me that we had to Let God have His way. This was one time that I feel like had we intervened then your heart would have been spared from being broken."

What did she mean by my mama's heart would have been spared? Had she found out about the other woman and if so why wasn't she acting like it? She was still walking around like everything was ok. I didn't realize that

I had been crying until I felt a tear drop on the hand that was covering my mouth.

Easing away from the door I made my way to my bedroom and closed the door. I didn't know if I was crying tears of joy or if these were tears of sadness for her. I knew that whatever was going on it was only going to get messier and I just prayed that God would keep us covered.

I reached inside of my purse to get my phone as I kicked off my sneakers and jumped on my bed. Kammy wasn't home yet and I had to get myself together before she got here just in case I had to step in for Mommy. I was so impatient as I waited for James to answer his phone.

"Waddup doe?" James said as he picked up on the third ring. Lord this little country boy had my heart skipping beats every time I heard his voice. No one knew that he and I had started a long distance relationship and we wanted to wait and tell our parents together when they came to my graduation in a few months.

"Drew isn't my real dad!" I blurted out. There was no easy way to pour this cup of tea.

"What?" he said as I heard the basketball in the background bouncing rapidly away. I knew then he had stopped his basketball game to make sure he had heard me correctly.

"I just heard my mother and grandparents talking about it in her office. I didn't mean to eavesdrop and as I was walking away I heard Grandpa say it."

"Wow." Was all he said. I knew he was in a state of shock just like I was a few moments ago.

"How do you feel about it?" he asked me once he got his thoughts together.

"Honestly I'm excited and happy. Like I told you before, I knew that I didn't have a connection with Drew and I always wanted that relationship. But I would always get what I needed from Bryce."

"Well you know that I understand that. The relationship that I yearned to have with my mother Monica I got once I met Nia for the first time." James had let me in on everything that he went through with his family when I first met him and you wouldn't know that Nia wasn't his biological mother if he hadn't told you.

That's the same way I felt about Bryce. He was so loving and connected to me and my sister that you would think that we were his. Now I knew why.

"Should I tell them that I know?" I asked.

"Pray about it first Ave. You don't want to do anything before it's time. Trust God through it all ok?"

This was why I loved James so much. He was a young man after God's own heart and he always gave the best advice.

"Ok I will. Just keep us in prayer please." I said to him.

"You already know I will. Call me later this evening so I can get back to practice. Coach just got here and I'm not trying to do anymore suicides today." He laughed.

"I'll call you after I finish my homework and Kam is in bed."

"Bet. I love you." He said smiling and causing me to blush.

"I love you too bae." I said before hanging up. I would do what James suggested and just pray about the situation. Either way I had a good feeling that things would work out. I just had no clue that things would get hell fire hot before they cooled off.

Chapter Seventeen

Jewel

To say that I was shocked would have been an understatement. I had no idea that Avery knew about what I had done all of those years ago and I was so worried that she would hate me or look down on me for it.

"It's ok Mommy. I don't look at you as a bad parent or woman because of what happened. We all fall short of the glory daily but we can't dwell in that or it will consume us. We must pray and keep seeking God through it all. I may be young but I know that a lot of times people drive themselves crazy about something that they have done and God has already forgiven them. They just fail to forgive themselves. It's time for you and Uncle Br-I mean Dad to forgive yourselves and move forward." I said.

"Where did you come from?" I laughed. I was so surprised to see her handling this the way that she was.

"So you're not mad at us for keeping this from you?" Bryce asked her.

"No. I understood why it was a secret for so long. I'm just glad that it's out in the open now so we all can move forward." She said as Kammy came and sat in her lap looking confused.

"What's wrong baby?" I asked my little princess.

"So you are my real Daddy?" she asked looking over at Bryce.

"Yes that's your daddy Kam." I told her waiting on her response.

"And Mr. Drew is my step daddy?" my poor baby was confused and it showed all over her face.

"Yes." Avery responded for me because the lump that just formed in my throat would not allow me to speak. God knows that I didn't know what I would do if Kammy took this harder than Avery. She was so young and the last thing I wanted was for my indiscretions to haunt or hurt either of my children.

"Since you are my real Daddy does that mean that you will be taking us to Disney World like Mr. Drew promised he would?" she said with the biggest smile on her beautiful face. Her eyes sparkled like never before when she looked at Bryce and that gave me a little bit of hope that everything would work out eventually.

I watched as Kam got out of her sister's lap and walked over to Bryce and wiped the tear that was about to fall from his eye.

"Daddy are you ok?" she asked him in her little sweet innocent voice. She seemed to be taking this way better than I had imagined. The sparkle in his eye at this moment didn't even compare to the one he had when he first saw each of them after they were born. Although he couldn't show it to the world because this was our secret I knew exactly what he was feeling.

"I am now baby. I am now." He said as she hugged him as tight as her little arms would allow.

"So can we go?" she asked again. I knew she wasn't about to let that trip pass her by.

"Let me and your mother talk about it but I don't see a problem with it." He said making her year.

"YAYYYYY!" she hollered as she ran up the steps.

"I'll let the two of you talk." Avery said.

Standing up I walked over to her and held her close. "I love you so much mommy and we will get through this as a family. Drew will reap what he has sown don't you worry." She said as she let me go and headed up to her room.

Chapter Eighteen

Kammy

I couldn't wait to tell my dolls Serena and Victoria about us going to Disney World. They were going to be just as excited as I was. We were gonna see Mickey Mouse and even my favorite Elsa and Oloft! Running into my room I got them out of my bed and sat them up.

"I got something to tell you. My new Daddy is going to take us to Disney World!" I said looking at their faces smiling.

They smiled all of the time cause I was a good mother to them just like Mommy always made me smile. She was the best mommy ever and I didn't want to see her cry but that's all she seemed to do lately. I wish I could fix it so she could smile again.

I held up each of their outfits that I was going to take for them to get their approval and their smiles once again showed me they were happy about my choices for them.

"We are gonna have soooo much fun together. Just me, and Mommy, and Avey, and Daddy Bryce, and you too. But where is Daddy Drew going to be? I made one of my dolls say. I knew I was playing pretend but that question had me confused. My big sister would tell me. I loved Avery and she was always there for me just like Mommy was. I wanted to be just like her when I grew up.

Running in Avery's room I jumped in her lap as she sat on her bed listening to music.

"Hey what are you doing love bug? You should be getting ready for bed we have school in the morning."

"I know but Serena had a question." I said as Avery gave me a knowing look.

"Now Kam you know Serena can't really talk right?" she asked me. I knew that but it was fun to have someone else to talk to even if it was pretend. I told my dolls a lot of my secrets and I knew they would never tell a soul.

"Yes. But anyway. If our Daddy is Bryce what does that make Drew? Our uncle?" I asked her. I was happy that he was because sometimes Drew could be really mean to mommy and Avery and that would make me sad but I didn't know what this meant. Would Daddy Drew live with us, was Mommy and Daddy Drew still married? Would he still live here too? And what about those women at church? This was too confusing to me.

"Well Kammy that's kind of hard to explain but I will try. See Mommy and Drew are married but God blessed us with Bryce being our real dad. He knew that Bryce would love us and never hurt us."this made no sense to me.

"But if God knew our new Daddy would love and never hurt us why didn't he stop Mommy from marrying Drew so she could marry our real Daddy?"

"Sometimes we don't always listen to when God tells us to do something. We let other people influence our decisions and they may not always be good for us. Then after a while God will allow certain things to happen in order to remind us of what He told us to do before. It's up to us to ask for forgiveness for being disobedient and start listening to what God tells us. A lot of times it hurts when God gets on to us but He only does it because He loves us and was to give us His best."

"Just like when mommy has to spank me if I don't listen but then after my punishment she tells me she loves me still?" I asked. I remember breaking her China doll and tried to hide it under the bathroom sink. I told a fib and when she found it in my bathroom she gave it to me good.

Then later on she came and explained to me why she had to punish me but that didn't stop her from loving me. She wasn't mad because I broke it she was mad because I lied to her about it. Mommy said that everything that is done in the light will be dark or something like that. I couldn't remember but it sounded really smart.

"Just like that."

"Can I ask you something else?"

"Of course."

"Why do you hate Daddy Drew so much?" Before she could answer me I heard Mommy coming up the steps and telling me it was time for bed. I kissed and hugged my big sister and climbed down to go in my room. I was sleepy. Today had been a busy day for this six year old.

Chapter Nineteen

Avery

God knows I was not prepared to answer that question and I was so glad that He sent Mommy in the nick of time. Having to go down memory lane and try to explain my feelings to a six year old would have been tough. She barely understood what I tried to explain to her and there was no way that she could understand why I felt the way I did towards Drew. Shoot some days I couldn't understand why but slowly God was revealing things to me as I got older.

I didn't necessarily hate Drew but I had a strong dislike for him. As far back as I could remember I got this funny feeling whenever he was around. I never felt a connection and often times my grandparents would tell my mother that I was able to discern his spirit. It took me years to understand what that meant but now I did. I always knew Drew was not here with us because he loved us but I could never understand why my mother couldn't see it. Blinded by love maybe.

There were so any times that Drew could have been a great husband and father but whatever demons he had in him wouldn't allow it I remember the first time that he left me hanging. I was in the second grade and we had grilled chicken sandwiches for lunch. I never ate the school lunch because mommy would make it but this particular day she wasn't feeling well so I had to eat what was served.

At first bite I knew something was off but my little greedy tail was starving so I pushed through. By the time we made it back to class my stomach was feeling queasy and I knew that at any moment I was about to blow. Before the thought was complete I was emptying everything out that I had just put in. The nurse couldn't reach Mommy so she got the number for the church and called Drew.

"Yeah?" he answered like he was being bothered. For him to be a loving Shepard of a flock he sure didn't act like it on the regular.

"This is Nurse Rita and I have Avery here with me. She just left lunch and got really sick and needs to be picked up." she said. Now a normal loving father would have dropped everything but not him.

"So call her mother." he said like that was the only option she had to do. I could tell Nurse Rita was taken aback but she kept it professuonal.

"Well from my understanding she is a little under the weather herself that's why I called you."

"Hold on." he said trying to cover up the receiver but I could make out that he was talking to someone in the room with him. Sounded like a woman but her voice didn't sound familiar. After as few more seconds of the rustling and voices he came back to the phone sounding even more agitated than before.

"Someone will be to get her." was all he said before the line went dead.

Thirty minutes later I saw my Uncle Bryce rush in with a worried look on his face as he asked Miss Ann the front desk clerk where I was. Before she could answer he noticed me sitting in the corner with the trashcan in front of me. He rushed over to me and all I saw was love and concern for me. Something I never saw in my so called father.

"Come on pumpkin let me get you home." he said while picking me up in one arm and grabbing my backpack with the other.

That memory was just the first of many that I had of Drew not being there when I needed him. He never taught me how a man should treat a woman, he never made it to any of my recitals or school award ceremonies, he didn't even acknowledge us too much unless it was out in public and mainly around church. He was always saying little smart comments about my mother's weight and her self-esteem. I hated when he did that. But as I got older I just prayed more that God would open her eyes to what everyone around her already saw. Today may have been rough but it was definitely an eye opener. I just hate she had to go through so much pain.

Right before I turned off my light and got under my covers there was a knock at the door and a notification that I received a text. I ignored the text right then and invited whoever it was on the other side of the door to come in

"You OK pumpkin?" my mom asked as she came in and sat down beside me.

"Are you ok?" I asked her taking the focus off of me. I would never forget the time that she went into such a deep depression and wouldn't even get out of the bed. I just prayed that didn't happen to her again.

"Don't worry baby. I'm not going down that dark road again. I have peace in the middle of this storm right now. I just want to make sure my girls are ok." she said moving a stray curl from my face.

"Actually I'm better than I have been in a long time and Kammy will .be just fine. I had a talk with her earlier. It's just gonna be a little while before she really understands what happened but she's a smart girl. All she cares about is going to Disney World." I said as we shared a laugh.

"Get some rest baby. Tomorrow will be eventful to say the least." she said getting up and kissing me on my forehead

"Do you want me to go with you?" I asked. If we thought today was fireworks then we knew tomorrow would be World War III.

"Laila Ali, Jr I can handle tomorrow." she giggled calling me by the name that she had given me after a fight I had one year at school. It wasn't right to beat that girl like that but God in heaven knows she tried me to the max.

I didn't know everything that was going to go down

tomorrow but I knew that if Drew showed up as scheduled it was about to go down.

"I love you Mommy."

"I love you so much more my baby." she said closing my door.

I looked down at my phone to see my goodnight text from James as I replied I couldn't help but to smile as the feeling of unexplainable joy took over my being.

Chapter Twenty

Drew

I woke up sore from the activities of the previous night. Once we got everything under control Constance made me feel like the man that I was. I looked over at her sleeping peacefully and though her body was calling me like that old school classic by R. Kelly I knew that we didn't have time. I had a little over an hour to get to the attorney's office downtown so that I could get those papers signed and my money be transferred.

Before hopping in the shower I got Constance up so that we could be ready on time. Had I let her just continue to lay there we would have definitely been late. That's one thing that Jewel didn't play and that was being on time anywhere she went. Constance was another story. She took forever to get ready no matter how much time in advance she had ready

Once we had gotten dressed I swung by McDonald's for a quick breakfast, Constance's treat of course, and we headed to the office. The email said that his office opened at 9am so I was going to be there on the dot. The parking lot was empty except two vars that were parked in the space right our front. I saw the secretary walk to the door to unlock it just as Constance and I were stepping out of the car. Hopefully by noon the fund would be transfered and we could be on our merry way.

"Good morning can I help you?" smiled the secretary. She was a young white lady who put you in the mind of that stalker woman who was after Beyoncé's husband in that movie Obsessed. She was nice on the eyes and I guess I was staring too long because Constance cleared her throat.

"Oh um I'm here to see Mr. Andrews." I told her

trying to regain my composure.

"Do you have an appointment?" she asked me as she at down to her computer to pull up the calendar.

"Well not exactly. I received an email about a week ago stating I just needed to come and sign a document by today. I just got around to seeing it late last night so I rushed in to get it done before I left town." I explained.

"Oh yes. Mr. Webber. Give me a few moments to pull those documents and I'll get Mr Andrews for you." she said. Her attitude seemed to change from when we first walked in but I guess the look Constance was giving her made her uncomfortable.

I was so anxious to get this show on the road that I couldn't sit still. It seemed like forever before the secretary returned and asked us to follow her. We ended up at the end of the hallway where we entered the office of a much older gentleman. He looked to be around his early sixties but his body looked to be well kept. He had dark skin the color of night with salt and pepper hair. I was tall so he had to be around my height or an inch or two taller. Life as an lawyer must have been good to him.

"Good morning Pastor." he said as his eyes shifted from me to Constance. Had I been thinking I should have left her in the lobby until this was over. I really didn't care that people knew about her now but I didn't want this to affect getting this money. Just as I was kicking myself internally he opened the manilla folder on his desk.

"I just need your signature on these two pieces of paper and everything will be complete." he said and I couldn't help the grin that spread across my face. I'm sure I looked just like the Grinch who stole Christmas with all of my teeth showing.

I signed on those dotted lines so fast as if my life depended on it and in a way it did. This was about to be the new beginning that I had been waiting on for almost twenty years. I knew God may not come when you want Him but

He's always on time.

"So now what?" I said as I handed him back the papers.

"Give me just one moment so I can get this information over to the bank." he said clicking on his keyboard then picking up his phone.

"Everything is a go." he calmly said giving me a broad smile. But something wasn't right. I felt Constance grab my arm holding it tight and she was smiling from ear to ear but something had suddenly sucked all of the air out of the room and I didn't k ow what it was but I knew it wasn't about to be good.

Before I could stand up the office door opened and in walked Jasmine.

"What on earth are you doing here?" I yelled. Just the sight of her made me sick to my stomach now that she was no longer needed. I only played this game with her because she had the info I needed and she was able to show me the side of her Jewel didn't have.

"So this is how you do? I help you get all of the information you need in order for us to make a come up and once you get it you leave your son and I out to dry?" by now her face was red and stained with tears. If I cared enough I probably would have tried to comfort her but I didnt.

"Man Jasmine you knew what it was from the jump. You couldn't have been that stupid to think that I wanted to leave one insecure woman and leave with the next." I said.

"Insecure?" she said like she was oblivious to that fact.

"Some days I didn't know who was worse you a or Jewel. Jewel had issues with herself and you on the other hand had issues with her. Everything I turned around it was 'Jewel this and Jewel that'. We could never focus on us even if there was to ever be an us because you were just as bad." I schooled her. Jasmine may have been a good fit for me but she wasted too much time trying to compete with my wife to show me how down she was for the cause, that she couldn't see her own insecurities.

After a few years I was done and when I stumbled across a document that said if I stayed until my 10th anniversary as Lead Pastor we would receive twenty million, I knew Jasmine had no idea. If she did she would have told me. I still had to play the game though because if I walked out on her completely she wouldn't hesitate to let Jewel in on it and I would be left with nothing.

"But I love you Drew. Your son loves you." she could have gotten an Oscar for this performance.

"My son? Oh you mean the one who doesn't share my DNA?" she had no clue that I had gotten her son tested a few months back on the advice of Constance just to make sure we could be completely done with her after everything was done.

Constance had a feeling DJ wasn't mine and I was

so glad that I got it done. Had I not she would have really been in my pockets. The look on her face let me know that she didn't have a comeback for this one because she was busted.

"Yeah that's right tramp. I made my man get that ugly little boy tested. You won't trap this one cause he came into some money." Constance stepped in. Just as Jasmine charged towards Constance the door flew open and I heard,

"Had I known it was going to be another WWE match so early I would have brought me some popcorn." It was Jewel.

Chapter Twenty One

Drew

This was all bad. How did she even know that I was here? I looked over at the lawyer and knew that this must have been planned. He sat there in his seat unbothered by the whole thing. But one thing I did know was that there was nothing anyone could do once those papers were signed and the transaction was complete. I was the only one who had access to that new account and could care less how anyone felt about it. That thought alone made me smile as I sat down in the chair next to Constance. She must have been thinking the same thing because her face held the same smirk that mine did.

I looked at Jewel and in 24 hours she looked so different. Her face held this glow that I had never seen. The confidence that illuminated from her was radiating and I found it breathtaking. Fine time for me to be thinking all of this while I was about to walk out on her. I couldn't front though, in all of the years of us being together I had never seen her look this good.

"Look at you. I guess you can clean yourself up nice." I said admiring her. The sundress she had on complemented her skin tone, her hair was flowing down her back in lots of curls, and she even had light makeup that brought out a side of her I had never seen. She must have had on one of those girdles that held everything in place because her body was stacked.

"She has always cleaned up nice you just never took the time to notice." I heard Bryce say walking in with a smug look on his face along with Jewel's parents and her brother Chris.

"What is this, a family reunion? Bryce you're not family so why are you here. Why are any of you here?

There is nothing anyone can do now. I just signed everything that's needed in order to receive that inheritance so you all are late." I said standing up to get ready to leave.

"You know what? After all of these years you still don't pay attention to details." Jewel said walking over to the desk.

"What are you talking about Jewel?" I asked tired of the merry-go-round that we were on. I wanted to know why everyone was here but no one was looking nervous or flipping out over the information I had just given them. You would think that she would be losing her mind to know that I had walked out of her life with all of her family's money and my new woman.

"Did you even bother to read what you were signing? I used to always get on to you for not reading things before you signed them." she said handing me the papers that I had just held in my hands not even ten minutes ago.

"Go ahead and read Drewsey."

All of my life I was told not to go signing papers without reading them in their entirety. I looked down and started reading just as Constance stood over my shoulder to see what it said. She too had warned me but we all know ow I don't take heed to warnings like I should. At the very top of the page I saw the words "Divorce Decree" and at the bottom was both mine and Jewel's signatures. I had just unknowingly given my wife a divorce.

"Ha. OK I see. Well that's one thing I won't have to worry about later on down the line. Come on baby we got money to blow and a happy life to live." I grabbed Constance by her hand ready to leave.

"Well you two have a nice life. I hope you have a nice savings or a good job, Constance is it?" Jewel said stopping me in my tracks. She may have gotten one over on me with the divorce but I had her with the money being transferred.

"What do you mean by that?" I was getting heated now because I was ready to go. Everything was signed so I no longer needed to be here but I needed to know what she was talking about. Something just wasn't right.

"What she means is that money you thought you were going to get transferred into that account she didn't know about, won't be transferred after all. So whatever savings you have you may want to spend it wisely." My father in law said. I felt like he was just blowing smoke out of his behind.

"That's where you're wrong old man. I just signed for that transfer to hit the new account didn't I Mr. Andrews?" Checkmate. I thought until Jewel shook her head and held up that other piece of paper. It was indeed a money transfer slip but the account number was for an account that I had never seen before.

"How di-" I started to ask before I was interrupted by Bryce.

"You never could hold your liquor well. Two drinks in and you will tell everything that you know and the next day remember nothing that happened. When you left to go to Atlanta the other week something in my spirit told me that I needed to give you a call. So I did. You were so tore up I was surprised that you could even speak. I thought God was leading me to call and check on you so that I could pray but He led me right to you confessing." he said bringing that night back to my remembrance.

*****

Jasmine and I had just gotten in from the club and were about to have a party of our own. Her son was gone and I knew that this was the last time that I would be with her in this way. I rarely drank anymore but since I knew this was the end I decided to go out with a bang.

We were throwing back shots and Jasmine had fired up something that she wrapped as soon as we hit the door.

Now drugs wasn't my thing but whatever it was had given me a contact so good I felt like I was floating. Whatever she put in the air mixed with that liquor had me feeling right.

Hours had passed and we were still going at it when my phone rang. I looked at my screen to see it was Bryce calling. I figured that he was calling to let me know that Jewel was worried cause it had been at least four days since I talked to her.

"What's up my boy?" I said as I watched Jasmine wind her body in front of me. I swear when I got to heaven I knew i was going to have me a couple of angels doing these moves. I burst out laughing at my own private joke as I heard my boy ask if I was ok. I didn't realize I had accidentally put my phone on speaker and Jasmine answered for me.

"He's fine Bryce and when he gets this money we will be even better." she laughed as I smacked her on her behind.

"What's she talking about? What money?" he asked. Now had I been sober none of this would have gone down no matter if he was my boy or not, but truth serum called Gin made me sing like a canary.

"Man she talking about that inheritance money from Jewel's folks. I contacted the lawyer to let him know we were changing the account that it was supposed to be deposited to because our account had gotten hacked. He said that he needed Jewel to sign the form to authorize it and that he was going to send it over to me right? So boom when he did I got ole girl to sign Jewel's name on it."

"Who is Ole girl?" Jasmine yelled in the background.

"Shet up and mind yo' bizzniee!" I yelled and fell out laughing cause I sounded just like my boy Lil Scrappy.

"Come on man are you serious?" Bryce asked me. If I didn't know any better I would have sworn this dude was sounding mad.

"You mad or nah?" I fell out laughing again.

"Yo I'm done. This is where I draw the line. Had I known own all these years that this is what you were on I would have never let you get close to her!" he yelled.

"He big mad now baby." Jasmine said.

"Yeah he is. It sounds like to me that you trying to be in ya feelings. Go ahead and tell it but when you do just know that you gonna have to tell everything. You helped me with most of it." I warned.

"Nah this is all you. I may have known about the women but not this." Bryce corrected.

"Who do you think my wife is going to believe? Her husband or someone who has a little crush on her?

That's alright though. When I'm long gone maybe she will let you dry her eyes." I said and hung up on him.

"That's right baby. You told him." Jasmine said to me as she sat on my lap and blew a cloud of smoke into my face.

****

There was nothing that I could do about what was being said because now I remembered it as clear as day.

"So I came clean with Jewel and her family. I let them know everything. I ran into her dad one day at the store and that's when I let him know that I needed us to all sit down before you got back. He thought because I was in town you were home as well."

"But when I called my daughter to confirm what Bryce had let me in on she told me that you were still out of town. I always knew that you were up to no good but after you got married I had to leave in God's hands. I knew sooner or later all would be revealed." Her father spoke finally.

I couldn't help but to bust out laughing to keep myself from crying.

"After all of these years of serving the Lord and blessing His people He does this to me? It was me that was laying hands. It was me that prophesied to the lost ones."I screamed.

"And it's gonna be you that bust hell wide open if you don't get right with God. For real. You been playing all of these years and your time has finally come." Her mother said. I didn't even know that this lil boy chest having woman was still alive.

"Sit cho lopsided chest having self down somewhere!" I yelled as Jewel started raining haymakers on me like she was a dude. One punch hit me square in the jaw and I felt the bone crack. You would have thought that jab would have made her stop but it didnt. I even tried to get a few locks in of my own but what did I do that for? As soon as I brought my hand back to slap the taste out of her mouth I felt like a heard of elephants were jumping on me. That's how hard her father, brother, and Bryce were connecting those blows. After what seemed like forever I just gave up and let the darkness consume me.

Chapter Twenty Two

Avery

I was on the phone with James as Kammy played in her room. We had just gotten home from school not too long ago and I made sure that we had a snack and completed the little bit of homework we both had. School was ok today all the way up until I got on the bus. This one girl named Onika that went to our church just made it her business to let everyone in on what had happened at church the day before. I guess she thought she was going to make me cry but I wouldn't give the enemy the satisfaction of seeing me bothered.

My mama always said that the enemy doesn't know that he has you unless you show him that you are bothered. Once he gets the reaction out of you that he was seeking then he knows where to keep hitting you at. But as long as he doesn't know he can't use it against you. But please believe he will try something else.

This girl talked for about twenty minutes giving her account of what happened and I couldn't do anything but laugh to keep from punching her in the face. This nut had the nerve to say that her mama heard Drew was sleeping with one of the mothers for her social security check. At this point things were just comical and over the top.

"Man what you say?" James asked me while I filled him in. He was laughing so hard the boy couldn't even breathe.

I giggled at the sound of his voice. No matter how I felt he could always make me feel better with his encouraging words and laughter. I just prayed that if it was God's will we would always be in each others lives. With so much hell going on around us one would think we would be broken down but the power of God is so amazing. He will put people in our lives to help us through. James was definitely a Godsend and I didn't want to let him go.

"I turned around and in my Kevin Hart voice asked, 'Are you done?' My eyes were bucked and everything like his was and everybody fell out." I laughed as I remembered the look on her face. She didn't say another word for the rest of the ride.

"I would have died laughing. But for real though I'm glad that you're feeling better. You know I hate to hear you cry and be upset. Especially if I'm not there to be able to comfort you." he said seriously. This was what I loved about James. He was so caring. His biological mother Monica had just died not too long ago and here he was worried about me. He always put others feelings first. James was just unselfish like that.

"I know Bae but I'm good. After talking to my mother and my dad last night and seeing her OK I feel better. Kammy seems to be OK so I'm good." I told him.

"This still trips me out that Bryce is your real dad.

Do you know how that happened?" he asked.

"Well when a woman and a man get naked-" I started but was interrupted.

"For real Ave? You tried it." James said trying to sound serious but I could hear the smile in his voice.

"Hey you asked." I laughed.

"You know good and we'll what I meant."

"We haven't sat down and discussed that part yet. I mean I know it wasn't planned but I haven't asked how it happened. I was born before they got married but Kammy is only six. I'm sure they will explain it one day." I said hearing a series of car doors slamming. I ran to my window to see my mom, dad, grandparents, and Uncle Chris coming into the house.

"Lord what done happened now?" I said more to myself than to James.

"Baby what's wrong?" I knew he was on high alert so I had to calm him down before he got all worked up.

"I don't know. My mom and grandparents just pulled up slamming car doors. Let me go find out what is going on and I will call you back in a few minutes ok?"

"OK babe I'll be waiting. Everything will work out for His glory. I love you." James is just too sweet.

I blushed as I told him I would call him back and that I loved him too before heading down stairs. Lord please be with us.

Chapter Twenty Three

Jasmine

Once the fight broke out at the lawyer's office and I found out that all of my hard work was in vain I grabbed my son's hand and got out of there as fast as I could. Everyone was so wrapped up in what was going on No one knew I had gone. I had to get out of there because I was numb.

My hands were shaking and it was getting harder to breathe every time I tried to inhale. Almost twenty years, four abortions, and one child later and still I had nothing to show for it. Everything my mother spoke over me as a little girl was coming to pass. When she told me that I would never be anything she was right. From as long as I could remember that's all I heard from her. Whenever my father decided to come around he cosigned right along with it. That's why when I made it out of high school and got into college I just knew I had proved them wrong only to find out they still thought I was a nobody.

"Look at me." My mother Adonna said to me one day. I was twelve years old at the time.

"You will never amount to anything. If you don't have a man to spend all of his money on you then you don't have nothing."

I looked around our small two bedroom trailer and it was filthy. Outdated furniture, clothes thrown about with beer and liquor bottles thrown about.

"I guess you're a nobody too then." I mumbled. I swear I thought I said it low but I guess I didn't say it low enough because the next think I knew I was being slapped so hard across my mouth I lost all feeling in my entire face.

"So you think you cute huh? I got a man. He takes

good care of me. You know what I don't have to explain anything to you. I'm grown and this is my house. Since you want to speak your mind you need your own house!" she ranted as she went about packing clothes.

I watched her as she got all of her things together, grabbed her keys to her little beat up Honda Accord and bounced. That was the last day that I saw her.

How does a mother just up and leave her twelve year old daughter like that. I hadn't even experienced my menstrual cycle yet and here I was raising myself. From that day forward I was on my own doing what I had to do to survive by any means necessary. If that meant tricking to keep the lights on and food in my belly that's what I did. I even had to be at the beck and call for the rent man. He knew my mama was gone but he said that if I made sure to take care of him like she did then I could stay there. It made me sick every time I did it but it also in a strange way made me go harder in school. I figured if I got good grades then I could go to college and have somewhere nice to stay for free. I wouldn't have to stress any longer about that.

When I got my acceptance letter to Spellman I just knew I was going to make it. I didn't have to give my body away because I had to now it was just cause I wanted to. I didn't go into school hating Jewel when I met her she was actually really sweet but then her feelings towards herself pissed me off to no end.

Here I was independent since I was a child with no one to love and she had both of her parents and a brother that loved her unconditionally. All of the boys from the surrounding colleges found something in her that she didn't know she possessed and she didn't have to give up anything for them to like her. They just did.

After our first semester Bryce and Drew started coming around more and they had started to build a good friendship. I could tell in his eyes that he wanted more but she was interested in Drew. She said there was just something about him that she wanted to learn about him. I was livid! How was it that this frumpy homebody had all of the attention but I had to open my legs to get someone to look at me?

So I plotted. Something would come up that would make me be the one to stand out a low and behold she opened up to me about her inheritance. I knew the perfect person to help me pull it off. I could give him all of the information he needed and in return earn his love and respect. At least that's what I thought. Whenever he got money from Jewel he would keep me laced too. He filled my head up of us being together and I honestly thought in some sick kind of way that I would have my happily ever after one day.

I was so excited when I found out I was pregnant by Drew the first time but that all came to an end once I told him. The first and last thing he said to me was to get rid of it. And that was that. I was so cared he would leave me if I didn't so I did it just to make him happy. I couldn't take someone else walking out on me.

When it came out that Jewel was pregnant a year later and she was keeping her baby the hatred for them both grew even stronger. How could he allow her to keep hers but not mine? But once he explained why she had to in order for their plan to work I softened a bit. Year after year, promise after promise, abortion after abortion. It seemed to be never ending.

Drew was the master manipulator. Satan in the flesh but Jewel couldn't see it. Bryce tried giving her hints without his boy knowing but it was no use. It wasn't until I got pregnant with DJ and he moved me into my apartment in Atlanta that I thought he was finally coming around. I knew that DJ wasn't his but I had no idea he would test him behind my back. Now here I was now all of these years later still with nothing. Adonna was right I would never be nothing. So it was time to end this.

I got up from the bed of the hotel room and went over to the refrigerator to get out DJ's sippy cup. I filled it up as he watched tv. I walked into the bathroom and pulled out my prescription bottles of Ambien and Oxycontin. I took every last Oxy that I had which was about twenty pills and swallowed them down. Next I crushed up the all of the Ambien and put them in DJ's cup making sure to mix them in really good. I wasn't going to be like my mother and abandon my child, I was taking him with me.

I didn't know if God would or He wouldn't forgive me for everything but I asked anyway. I lay beside him as he drank his juice and watched SpongeBob until his little eyes got heavy and his breathing became shallow. When his little arm fell to his side and his cup hit the floor I was emotionless. Maybe because the drugs I had taken were starting to work on me as well. I watched his chest rise and fall until he took his last breath then I closed my eyes to be with my son.

Chapter Twenty Three

Jewel

I slammed my car door shut and headed into my house. I had tunnel vision after I blanked out on Drew in Mr. Andrews' office. All of these years of pent up anger, hurt, and frustration was let loose when Drew got flip about my mama. He knew her condition and to stand there and make fun of her sent me over the edge. I was like a raging bull and all I saw was red. I hadn't noticed that my parents, brother, and Bryce were following behind me until I tried slamming the front door only for it to be stopped by a hand.

"Whoa Tyson!" I heard my dad say. If I hadn't still been so amped up I may have laughed but I was done.

"I like your nerve Ali. And you had Holyfield and Mayweather right along with you." my mother said laughing. I wanted in on the joke cause I didn't find anything funny at the moment.

"Boy what are you doing?" my father asked my brother Chris. He was looking inside the DVD player and the movies on the entertainment shelf.

"I'm trying to see if she watched Hustle and Flow last night." he replied confusing everyone but Bryce. He must have caught on because he was laughing so hard he was crying.

"What are you talking about?" my father asked.

"She had to have been watching that movie cause she beat down Drew like DJ did Skinny Black. You heard Whoop That Trick didn't you?" he said falling out laughing.

"You are so corny sometimes. Fix it Jesus." I said but I couldn't help but to crack a smile.

It was something that broke on me the minute Drew's jaw broke on him. God forgive me but I got him good.

"Well at least you are smiling now." My mother said.

"I'm so sorry for what was said about you Mommy. That hurt me to my soul." I told her.

"Oh hush that up. You can't control what someone says but I'm glad to know that you will go to war for your mama."

"All day every day." I said hugging her.

"I'm glad that everyone is breathing a little easier now but for some reason I don't think that this is over with Drew. My spirit is telling me that he is not done messing with you but God still sits high and looks low." My Dad said.

"I was feeling the same thing but I didn't want to speak on it just yet. He's not gonna let this go. His ego is bruised right along with his face." Bryce said as Avery came down the stairs.

"Mommy are you ok? I heard you slamming the car doors. Hey Papa and Nana. Hey Uncle Chris. Hey Daddy." Avery said.

The look on my parents face was priceless and they lit up like Christmas trees. I knew they were excited about the girls finally knowing and I also knew they were wondering what would become of Bryce and I. I was excited to know that my man of God was finally in my life to stay.

"I'm fine baby. Everything is fine and we have to get ready for graduation next week. James and his family will be here and we have so much to focus on." I told her as she smiled harder than ever at the mention of that little boy James. I was glad that she had him as a friend.

Chapter Twenty Four

Drew

I woke up in the hospital hooked up to all of these monitors. My body felt like I had been hit by an eighteen wheeler and then the driver put the truck in reverse and hit him again. It took me a minute to remember what happened and when the realization came back to me like a flood. The events of the day just made me even angrier to know I was laid up in this hospital and nothing was in my account.

"Damn!" I yelled out in frustration. I hit the side of the bed and the pain almost took my breath away. Once I got myself together I hit the pump on the Morphine drip that was beside the bed and saw a piece of paper on my lap.

I opened it and noticed it was Constance's handwriting. I was shocked that she wasn't here but I continued to read it.

Drew,

Something has to give. I won't make this long because I know that you are in some serious pain. Jewel and her folks gave you a serious beat down! Lol!! I didn't know she had it in her but I guess she was a woman scorned for real.

Well rest assured that I'm not scorned in any shape, form, or fashion but I am tired of this back and forth with Jewel. She is a smart one. I will give her that. You were so dumb and this plan we had was fool proof. Or so I thought. You were certainly the fool this go round.

All of these years you know I have been real patient and even make my own living but it's time for me to retire as promised. I don't know what to tell you but if you don't come up with enough coins to make me happy then I'm done. The kids and I will walk and find someone else to take care of us. Maybe Bryce has a relative cause that brother is shole nuff fine! Ha! Yes God!! Now I see why she went running to him and ended up conceiving his two daughters. Oh that's right you didn't know that Avery and Kammy were his daughters and not yours huh? A blind man could see those girls look like him and they loved him way more than they loved you.

I bet you're wondering how I knew about that little bit of info huh? Constance always has her ways to get the info that she needs. Maybe if you come through with some money I'll share that with you then. Get me my money Drew or forget my number. You have three weeks or it's a wrap. And please don't get cute on me because there is some info that you don't want me to let out of the bag now do you? Play wit it if you want to. Toodles boo!

Constance <3

My life as I knew it was over. There was no way that I could come back from this and I just prayed that Constance wouldn't make good on her threats. There was just some things that didn't need to get out. One thing I did know though is if I didn't come through like she wanted I was going to have to shut her up permanently.

Chapter Twenty Five

Avery

It was finally graduation day! I was so excited that I couldn't even sleep last night. Not only was I about to enter into adult hood and take the next step towards my future but I was going to share this moment with the love of my life. I couldn't wait to see him after the ceremony and get this big surprise that he had for me.

I heard the text notification go off and I smiled knowing it was from him. I opened it to see his smiling face followed by a scripture and a few words of encouragement. He always knew what I needed and when I needed it. This must have been how my dad felt about my mom all of these years. I'm just glad that he held on until God opened that door for them to fully be together. They finally sat down the other night after my grandparents left and explained everything. I wasn't the least bit upset and it was truly a Kingdom relationship. I was in a happy place. Kammy still got a little confused when she called Dad by his name but we knew that it would take some time for her and he was so understanding.

"Come on baby girl!" my mother yelled. I grabbed my purse, cap, and gown and headed downstairs. It was that time.

"I'm so proud of you baby. We both are." She said with tears in her eyes.

"Don't cry Mommy. At least not yet." I said to her smiling.

"Ok but I can't make promises for later."

"I wouldn't expect you to."

My dad came downstairs with Kammy into and kissed me on my cheek. The look in his eyes told me that he loved me unconditionally and he was so proud of me. I

couldn't have asked for anything more as we walked out
the door as a family.

Chapter Twenty Six

James

Today was the day Avery graduated and I think I
was more excited than she was. She was feeling a little
nervous but I had already sent her a text to calm her nerves
a little. Avery would always ask me to send her a picture of
my smile when she needed reassurance on something. I
hated taking what the girls called selfies but I snapped a
picture of myself and sent it to her with a short prayer and
scripture.

"Boy every time I turn around you on the phone.
Why aren't you dressed yet? You know it's going to take
us some time to get over to the school, find a parking spot
and then walk in there and get a seat." My mother Nia said.

"Alright ma dang. I was just take a quick picture, you know yo boy done got cut up and looking good don't hate," I laughed as she threw a pillow at me.

"Hurry up! Oh and help JJ finish getting dressed too. Let me go to our room and make sure your daddy doing what he's supposed to be doing," she closed the door.

I helped JJ get dressed and I threw on my nice button up shirt and sprayed a splash of my cologne on. I was looking good with my nice fade and my little beard had come in nicely. I was looking like the younger version of my father which was a compliment. I took my phone off the charger and gestured for JJ to come on so we could check on the old folks and see what they were doing. After everyone was dressed we headed towards the school. The closer we got to the school the more my stomach started to cramp. Avery had been through so much and I was so proud of her. I wanted to make tonight special for her so my parents reserved a table at Ruth's Chris Steakhouse.

We were able to get a good parking spot and I know my mama was glad because she decided to wear five inch heels to a graduation. I already knew my dad put her up to it because he loved to see her in heels. My dad sent Mr. Bryce a text to see where they were sitting, they also had a good spot and Avery was able to see us from where she was sitting. I was so proud of her because she was graduating with honors. All of the honors student's had to sit towards the front.

"I'm so glad you guys could make it," Mr. Bryce stood up and shook my hand and then my father's.

Mrs. Jewel and my mother hugged and talked like school girls until the ceremony started. Bryce went all out and bought Avery all these balloons that spelled her name out and roses and here I was with my small little gift in my pocket. When they called Avery's name out we all got up hollering and screaming, everyone around us thought we were crazy but if they only knew what Avery had went through they would've been rejoicing with us too. I wanted to be the first to get to Avery after the ceremony so I started walking down a little early so I could have a quick moment with her. After the tassels were turned and the hats were thrown up in the air I raced down to grab and hug Avery.

"I'm so proud of you. Through it all you kept your head held high, now sky is the limit. I have a surprise for you tonight," I hugged her again. Before she could even ask what the surprise was Jewel grabbed her and hugged her as they both cried tears of joy. Avery hugged everyone and took pictures with her classmates and everyone said their goodbyes as we headed to Ruth's Chris. I pulled out Avery's chair and saw my mother smirk. I had a feeling she was on to me but time would only tell. We all ordered and enjoyed conversation and food, JJ was having a hard time with his little steak so I cut it up for him so he could eat it better.

"I'm going to miss all of you guys when I leave. I love you mommy and daddy but I'm gone miss James too. I mean we always talk on the phone but California is a long way and you are not going to be able to just drive to come and see me," I listened to Avery explain.

"Well I wouldn't say we will be too far," I reached in my pocket and pulled out the letter.

"What is that James?" Avery asked with a confused expression on her pretty face.

"I got accepted to USC too. So now we get to be together," I hand her the letter.

"What you mean be together?" Mr. Bryce looked at me.

"Daddy…"

"Mr. Bryce I wanted to tell you this face to face but I am in love with your daughter. We've been in a relationship for about a year now. I've seen her in her worse, and I've been there to pray her through it. And to take it a little further," I reached in my other pocket and pulled out a box and got on my knee.

"James what are you doing," I could hear my father saying and everyone else gasping for breath.

"Avery will you marry me?" I asked her as I held my own breath.

I watched as Avery looked at her parents with tears in her eyes. As I waited on an answer it felt like eternity and my hands started sweating. I wasn't sure if I could be rejected in front of all these people.

"Yes! Yes I'll marry you," she hugged me.

"Wait a minute son. Now don't you think you moving too fast? California is too far for the both of you really but definitely you," my dad fussed. I couldn't read the reaction on Avery's parents, they were speechless.

"Mommy, Daddy say something please. James has always been good to me, you know what kind of person he is."

"Avery baby I don't know about this. Bryce what do you think? I can't believe you guys are going to college together and then you hid your relationship from us and now you're getting married. This is way too much for one night," Jewel said.

"Ok let's all bring it back in here. Let me first start by saying that I had a feeling that you were dating Avery. It was many nights I stood outside your door and listen to you pray for her on FaceTime or even in your private time with God. I for one wouldn't want you to be with anyone else but Avery because I know she was raised in the ammunition of God. I am secure knowing that Jewel did a great job with you and Bryce you have always been influential in her life. I think we need to let them make this decision and trust God in this. They are both grown now, the only thing we are supposed to do is train them up," my mother said. After she said what she said I could see my dad and Avery's dad soften up some. Jewel even relaxed a little.

"James you are a great kid but you have to understand that Avery is my daughter, and she doesn't need another daddy in her life. I'm going to trust you not to bring any harm to her because if you do, you got to deal with me. Understood?" Mr. Bryce said matter of factly. It made me smile that she now had the father that she was supposed to have who really loved and cared for her.

"Yes sir."

"I can assure you that my son will take good care of your daughter. I wasn't always the best man that I could be, but once I let God completely have His way I became what I was supposed to be and that was the priest of my home," my father said.

"Well Jewel looks like we are planning a wedding," my mama said.

Chapter Twenty Seven

Kammy

It was the last day of school and I was so excited. As soon as school was over we were going to Disney World. I was happy that my friend Chelsea and JJ were going with us. We were going to have so much fun.

Jessica and Tamela were mad when I told them that I was going because they couldn't go. They always picked at me when they did something that I couldn't do. I bet they would want to be my friends when we got back to school.

The bell hadn't rang yet but the front office just called to let me know my Daddy was here. I was so happy that I didn't have to wait until the end of school to leave. Everybody else had a few more hours of school but not me.

I got my stuff and said by to my class, all except

Jessica and Tamela, and ran to the car. I hopped in and

buckled my seat belt.

"Hi Daddy!" I said smiling.

"You ready to go see Elsa and Oloft?" he

asked me.

"Yep! I can't wait. I'm going to tell Elsa all

about my room and maybe she will come visit one day." I

told him.

"That would be nice baby. Here call mommy and let

her know that I have you." He said handing me his phone.

"Yes hello?" Mommy said answering her phone.

"Hi Mommy!"

"Kammy?" she asked sounding like she didn't

know my voice.

"Yes it's me. Daddy picked me up early." I told her.

"Kammy. Bryce is still here he hasn't left to come get you yet." She said. Mommy didn't sound right.

"Not Daddy Bryce Mommy. Daddy Drew." I told her.

"OH MY GO NOOOOOOOOOOOOOO! BRYCEEEEEEEE!" she screamed as Daddy took the phone from me.

"Checkmate." Was all he said to her and I knew something was wrong. I don't think I'm going to Disney World.

To be continued........